# Hot Flashes

## 101 REASONS TO LAUGH AT LIFE

### SUE LANGENBERG

A Division of Windy City Publishers

Chicago, IL

*HOT FLASHES: 101 Reasons to Laugh at Life*

Second City Books
1935 S. Plum Grove Rd., #349
Palatine, IL 60067
www.secondcitybooks.com

Published in the United States of America

First Edition 2011

ISBN: 978-1-935766-09-4

Library of Congress Control Number: 2010941471

Cover Design by Wendy Barrett
Illustrations by Krista Wildermuth

This book is dedicated to all acquaintances
that I have either befriended or begot over the years.
You have all laughed either with me or at me,
but it is all good...

And to a special friend Jill Wagoner Johnson who had the nerve to die
before we were finished laughing...

# CONTENTS

The Calamitous Commode

A Checkered Background Check

Not a Chip Off the 'Ol Block**

A Friendly Financial Wet Blanket

A Dinosaur Named Who?***

A Map-less Male Worth Saving*

A New and Improved Hag-z! Scheme

The Face of Hagbook

A Gorilla-Sized Hot Flash, Probably

A Grandmother's Folly

A Resolution For Jack Sprat

A Seismic Event

A Leggy Situation

A Standardized Landfill

A Wolf in Sheep's Clothing

Ants in My Pants

Abetting the Rumor Mill

As Easy as Falling Out of Bed

Being the Fool That's Born Every Minute

Reaching the Whopper Threshold

Accomplishing Great Things Up the Suction Hose**

Calling All Humans

Chariot Race Moments of Today

Following the Yellow Brick Road

All in a Twitter***

The Local Chapter of Crabgrasses

The Life and Times of Wallpaper

Declaring Waterbeds a Wash

Diva and the Glue Factory

# CONTENTS

All That Glitters...

Forgetting About Alzheimer's

Form Follows Function

Giving Thanks to the Turkey in Your Life

An Elevating Idea for MS. Otis

Having a Handy Home Solici-Zapper

Here's Mud in Your Eye

Home Again, Home Again, Jiggity Jig

Bah Halloweenbug!

Horse Thieves of a New Age

In Praise of Procrastination

In Search of the Designer Parking Place

Banking on the Tooth Fairy***

Influenza and the Naked Lady

Just Desserts for the Finicky Eater**

Just Your Average GOSSIP

Two-timing the Clock

Laughing Just for Giggles

Leaping Into 'Feb-you-wary'

Liar, Liar, Pants on Fire!

Coming Clean on the Laundry

Literature of the Third Age

Making Noise About Men

Minding the 'Mentors' From My Discipline Square

Death By Chocolate

Mother Nature's Biggest Blunder Yet

Beware the Wrath of Hurricane Hag

Name-Dropping That Goes 'Thud'

Not a Frequent Flyer

# CONTENTS

Diet For an Old Hag

"O Phony Tree, O Phony Tree"

Occupation: Pigeon Lady

Playing the Board Game Called 'Gasopoly'

The Cankles Report

Recovering From 'Post Traumatic Checkbook Syndrome'

Practicing Sleepus Interruptus

Putting a Lid On It

Flunking Car Seat 101***

Shot in the Heart By Saint Valentine

Sleeping For Another Hundred Years

The Conspiratorial Lawnmower

Spring Cleaning the Family Genes

Getting the Skinny On Fat

Successful Failures in 2011

Paint the Town Pink!

That Dreadful "C" Word

It's the Bees Knees

Hats OFF to Hats OFF

The Blame Game

A Well-Adjusted Critter Getter

The Cure For Fatal Carpeting*

Having the Handy-Dandy Wife on Staff

Designer Furnace Filters and One Inch

The Hallmark of Success

Not a Happy Camper

The Invisible Raise

The Consummate Couch

# CONTENTS

Hot Headed About Cold Feet

Pick a Storm, Any Storm

The Life and Times of Cooties

Fashions For the Derriere Crevice

The Next Generation of Zeroes

The Stats Are In

If the Shoe Fits...

The World's Newest Profession

There's No Place Like Home

Toys R Them

'May Day' For the Flowerholic

Uncorking the Truth

The Work-At-Home Fantasy

The Nursing Home Swans

Dying to Laugh

Langenberg's columns have regularly placed in the HumorPress.com contest.
The above marked columns have won the following distinctions:

\* Finalist

\*\* Semi-Finalist

\*\*\* Honorable Mention

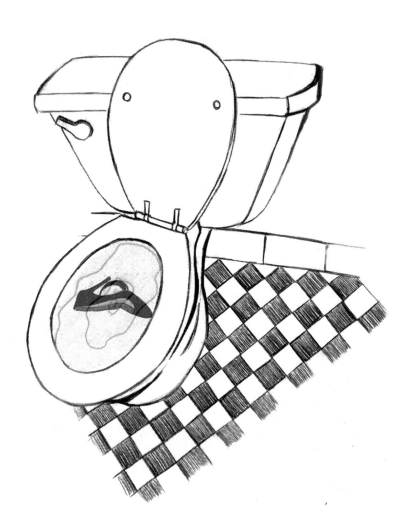

# The Calamitous Commode

There are some who say that their careers are in the toilet. I can understand that. I've had times in life when I thought my whole life was in the toilet. And those traumas would be triggered by something as ordinary as having a clogged pore.

My current problem, however, is that my upstairs toilet is in the toilet.

And so it occurred to me recently that I had better order a new one. The old one wasn't making the right swishing noises, the whirlpool of water wasn't going anywhere and I had to be a certified whirligig operator to get it to stop running. Along with that, there would be instructions to guests complete with x-rated gestures on how to operate the thing.

So when my last water bill looked more like an arrest warrant for assault on the city water tower, it was time to act.

As an addicted house design-o-phile, I get excited about changes. Granted, I'd rather have a new state-of-the-art kitchen straight out of the dream magazines. Or maybe a new brick terrace where my hag friends and I can sip from long stems and admire my newly landscaped rose garden.

But hey, I'll take a new toilet. It's a change, after all. So when the plumbers trudged in carrying the new box with gleaming porcelain, I was buoyant about the house upgrade, no matter how insignificant.

I envisioned a new toilet smiling and sparkling in its stylish bone color. And I would flush it and walk away like a normal person in the Third Age. My new toilet would make strong whooshy sounds, sing an entire stanza of "Anchors Away" then fall responsibly silent until its next use. Even the water bill people would celebrate and deliver a bill somewhere beneath room temperature.

"Ah, er," was the first indication from one of the plumbers that there

1

might be one small teensy, weensy problem. "I think the floor is sinking,"was his next sober observation.

But he pressed on and didn't burst my bubble yet. The house was still standing, and if I promised to call my handy dandy carpenter soon, all would be fine.

But the news got worse. "Ah, I don't think..." and he went on about how maybe the house wasn't still standing and that there was nothing left, in fact, to attach the new toilet to. So I was advised to wait for the new toilet and call my carpenter to prevent further damage meantime.

Had I waited longer, in fact, the old toilet – circa 1937 – would have eventually fallen through the ceiling. That would have been as timely as the clogged pore. Forget the brick terrace and the wine stems, my hag friends would have been in the living room below during that fateful occasion.

We would have had our noses in the air while engaging in proper conversation like who read what high brow literature lately, or how best to appreciate an upcoming art exhibition. Soon, however, we would lower our noses into shallow gossip about some daughter's mother-in-law and how she made a scene buzz buzz buzz.

But, "What's that noise?" would have immediately escalated into an emerging tumor in the ceiling followed by an ungainly crash to the couch below, narrowly missing one of my hag friends. There would then be a cloud of dust swirling around shards of porcelain everywhere. When the dust settled, there may have been a curious and confused cat peering through the new hole from above.

Sometimes life is in the toilet.

# A CHecKered BacKgroUNd CHecK

There are thorough background checks for everyone these days. Every time there are applications to fill out for anything, we are under microscopic scrutiny to prove that we are squeaky clean upright citizens that pulverize garden soil.

Just look at every job application. At the top is the regular stuff to verify a mailing address. It might currently be a box under a bridge. "How long at this address?" follows to determine residential stability. Well, maybe only a few weeks now after the house sold to fill the gas tank. The line to provide a phone number might also be blank after sacrificing the cell phone, land line and beepers to call teenagers from the bedroom to dinner. All those communications are grounded to a halt to buy this week's groceries.

Then comes the background information; "Are you a convicted felon, i.e. have you drooled in public in front of a bakery?" Well, no, but my dog left a nuisance in front of one 40 years ago. Oh-oh. With the "Please explain," space, I'll have to fess up that I didn't have a plastic bag with me. The ladies in the bakery never got over it, so I guess that defames my character and I won't be qualified for this job.

My favorite section of the background check is the part about personal references. With puffing peacock confidence, I proudly list three friends who are upstanding pillars of the community and can attest to my reliability. Then, I remember that I blew off one for dinner plans because I forgot to look at my calendar. I once smart-mouthed another friend because she didn't want to go to the same restaurant as I. My one remaining friend refuses to be seen with me in public because I once wore white after Labor Day.

3

So much for personal references.

It began with my first job as a teenager to waitress part time for a local restaurant. When I applied in person, the owner looked me over and asked about my background. At the time, I was only guilty of picking zits and holding the world's record for occupying the bathroom the longest. Luckily, times were less dependent on such checkered backgrounds.

If my sordid and misguided background flunks this paperwork, I can't imagine an aspiring presidential candidate who must endure an entire past rearing its ugly head. These days, squeaky clean is not enough. They must promise that they never wore diapers. To back up that claim, the spirit of a loving mother must rise from the grave, circle the network cameras and swear on a stack of baked cookies that her perfect child was born with Lysol surrounding the umbilical cord. Then, a kindergarten teacher somewhere must step forward and say that this child bypassed the bus and walked on water to get to the first day of school.

But then again, that kindergarten teacher may not pass her background check what with flaws and foibles all around.

About scandalous indiscretions, let's just say that all political candidates everywhere must prove that there have never been any DNA exchanges with another human being except the pizza delivery guy. Even then, there must be witnesses to prove that the delivery man lives in a Plexiglas bubble and donates his tip with white gloves to the homeless, backgroundless and Lysol products.

I actually applaud mistakes and indiscretions in life that make a checkered background. Who would want to wake up at aged 85 and realize that the only thing to be proud of is being the most boring human being on the planet?

# Not a Chip Off the 'Ol Block

**A** computer chip, that is. Somewhere along the line the dog and cat chips caught on in humans. And I was just beginning to grasp this marvelous chip thing so that our dogs don't run away or cats stray from their domestic mice.

Now I understand that whatever chips these pets have are inbred in humans. No insertion necessary. Hospital nurseries are noticing that newborn computer chips are already functioning underneath the umbilical cord.

The newborns now come out with a tiny remote in their little hands to guide the ceiling monitors to cartoons where monsters snicker at non-chipped parents and non-chipped parents snicker at science fiction where newborns have chips. By the time they learn to walk, they have already bypassed regular English and promoted themselves straight to text language. "H, Gma, how r u?"

I realized this after a visit from my five-year-old grandson. I picked up a few toys and noticed that my computer mouse was lying there dead, belly up. Rigor mortise had already set in on the four legs pointing to the ceiling.

Yes, I remember this enterprising kindergartener at the computer for a length of time. But I left the room after I carefully spelled "Teletubbies" for him. By the time I poured another cup of coffee and returned, the room was spinning with upgrades, program downloads and a big red dog was lounging on the couch. I think there was also some green monster peeking from behind the monitor.

The printer had been overloaded with about six inches of the most expensive photo paper to run off scanned graphics of a five-year-old hand, one tiny tic-tac-toe game in all colors of the rainbow and one set of ABC's in the smallest font on 25 sheets.  He was very proud of his accomplishment.  "C Gma?"

There was an inch of leftover photo paper, however, so he took online instructions to fashion an instant confetti gismo to celebrate along with the balloons that he conned me into buying at the store.  The one balloon that didn't pop still hovers over my computer.  It says "Class of '10."  That means that five-year-olds now graduate from "Outchipping Grandmothers with Chins 101."

The mouse innocently clicked into shock several times while I tried to recover my computer from a newfound virus.  My beloved Solitaire game had turned into something with colors that made no sense and the homepage was suddenly a pinball game where I couldn't log on until I got the bouncing ball safely into the letter "U" in my Word program.

And here I was impressed with how my computer did things like write, save and send.  I knew how to turn it on with gentle patience and off with stages of sleep.  Sending digital photos in between were for the advanced, but I finally got it.  Next time, I'll just ask a pre-loaded grandchild whose inborn chip can order cookies instantly via E-Dough.

I'm not sure what this newfangled Mother Goose chip looks like, nor the one that goes into dogs and cats.  I imagine, however, based on my grandson that human heads are now born larger to accommodate the chip size, probably in the texture of a sponge.  There are zapping arrows that operate between bulging eyes, bright screens and a very nervous mouse.

Part of that inborn chip is see-through, I notice.  It is located where an unruly cowlick is somewhere on top of the head.  If you look closely, you can see wheels turn, especially when a chipless grandmother asks a stupid computer question.

# A Friendly Financial Wet Blanket

I once had a friend who managed his finances like a scam-artist. If there were a free ticket, free ride or free dinner he would be right there as a social animal. If he had to hold his own like any other grown-up, however, he would prefer to stay home and calculate how he could live without water and electricity.

Sometimes, if he needed extra cash he would sell some personal belongings. The last time I saw his place, it looked more like a cell block. Otherwise, if he needed anything, he would "borrow" from friends, as if everyone were a lending library.

Managing finances with some frugal budgeting is an activity that most of us can relate to. Yes, I clip a few coupons and shop for the least expensive toilet paper.

But when it comes to a restaurant outing with friends, it seems more appropriate to leave the ledger sheet at home and generously offer whatever it takes to settle the bill. It has been called "going Dutch." And friends act this way around friends.

This financial wet blanket was otherwise an educated and harmless person who appeared to fit into any social gathering with light humor and a charming demeanor. He would tell the right jokes, laugh at the right quips and wit his way around everyone with an easy-going manner…until the restaurant tab came. Then he was suddenly in the bathroom.

The timing of his disappearing act took many years to perfect. Male friends from college remember their sports gatherings for drinks at the bar. Hardy har, flex the muscles and have another Bud, thank you. But when the tab came, the financial wet blanket was unavailable.

At dinner, if he were off guard from his disappearing act and the tab was delivered to near his plate, his jowls stiffened into rigor mortis. He eyed the tab as if the Bubonic Plague had invaded our table. While the rest of us would reach into our wallets and purses, his end of the table turned into a small accounting firm.

Clacking away with blurs of figures and quarter-figures, he would calculate who had the whatever special, exactly how much wine was consumed down to the molecule and whose dessert was untouched. Then he would do a complete background check on the waitress and assess minor offenses ("My salad was late"), then diminish the tip down to the last half-cent with, "Ok, you owe me that half-cent at the next dinner."

One time, the money was in order and stacked on the table. He was suspiciously the last one to leave. Then he quietly scarfed back the tip money that he had been forced to leave earlier with witnesses around. Honest!

Another time, a friend had some free theatre tickets. To prove to ourselves that he was a financial wet blanket, we rehearsed our mini-drama in the restaurant bathroom. She fronted me some cash so that I could pretend to pay for it across the table with grand flourish.

"Oh, here" (flutter the bills past his face), "I almost forgot to pay you for the ticket tonight."

"Why, thank you, Sue," she replied in hint-hint capitol letters. "I'll just hang onto the tickets until we get there," she said with megaphone clarity in his direction.

It was rigor mortis again.

His favorite restaurant scam is when someone takes out a credit card for the total while the rest of us contribute cash. We tallied later one time who paid for what, and were horrified to find that the generous credit card person had mostly paid for the pizza, of which the financial wet blanket consumed the most. That's when I declared that he was no longer a dinner friend.

I haven't seen him much these days, but notice that he has improved his station in life by befriending rich widows.

# A Dinosaur Named Who?

**A** friend admitted that she had way too much time at an airport recently. She had done her exercise walk and had removed her terrorist gear from her eye shadow brush. So she moseyed around to look in the shops with two "Ps" and an "E," or quaint, high-end shoppes.

It so happens that airports know when unsuspecting hags might have time to spare, so they place shoppes in strategic locations, like everywhere.

She had already bought me a charming purse, probably because she was embarrassed to be seen at the opera with me carrying denim. Or another one that collected cat hair that made everyone sneeze within a square mile.

So she handed me a cute little white box when I picked her up from the bus. It was a charming snow globe, not just any snow globe, one that had the famous dinosaur named Sue.

Funny, I shook it and confetti from my shredder swirled in a blizzard of pieces of my life, mostly bills. Once settled, I thought that I was looking in the mirror. How clever of her to bring me something where I resembled the famous, largest and heaviest dinosaur unearthed on record.

The face glared at me with a row of teeth that had obviously been flossed and brushed with great care. The mouth was completely open to see such, but then it was probably always open in her time to yak about the latest gossip concerning a sister-in-law's Tyrannosaurus brother whose sharp-toothed mother stomped off over a cliff after some other saurus-in-law who wouldn't stop…I guess dinosaurs had dysfunctional families, also.

Her bones bore traces of aspirin or anti-inflammatory medication to ease the pain of hillside exercise rituals, something that female dinosaurs had to do to keep their tails svelte, also to keep their mates home from roaming the countryside looking for like dinosaurs with lipstick and flossed teeth.

The dinosaur was named after discoverer Sue, though no one actually knows whether male or female. My marvelous little snow globe tells me that she is obviously a female because her hips are large enough to score a basketball hoop in one shot. With several hundred over-sized eggs to process, her varicose veins still remain, at least in my snow globe.

I peered into her face and, sure enough, there were several chins and gray wrinkles. She must have already gone into dinosauri-pause with the accompanying hot flashes to heat up an entire hillside with her fire-breathing discomfort. It looks to me like she was crabby on a regular basis, especially when a bone-scratching male dinosaur entered the scene. Her lengthy tail seems extraordinary, like maybe she flipped it around to warn others of her dinosauri-pause moods.

I was naturally inspired to look up this dinosaur named Sue to see how her life was from day to day. My first discovery was that she procrastinated most of her existence. Paleontologists would dispute this but certain dinosaurs, especially the ones in snow globes, developed a few words. One was "later" when it came to cleaning the saurus dwelling. She complained bitterly about having to do everything while all the male did was pick his teeth with tree branches.

She also seemed to have thrived in ages before luxurious digs with all the creature comforts a dinosaur could want, like state-of-the-art carnivorous kitchen tools to make instant meals fit for a queen.

My snow globe, however, indicates that she nested in a lap of comfort with expensive wine, good books and flowers to admire while saying, "later," to responsible tasks.

# A Map-Less Male Worth Saving

It is often noted that males who get lost refuse to ask directions.

Not to weigh in on any feminist food fight or anything, I imagine that it's because that pesky Y-chromosome doesn't want to be caught red-handed not knowing where he's going. Any male who has lost his way in life, even for a moment, might appear less a macho man. You can't flex your muscles, after all, while asking directions from perfect strangers.

When we women get lost, we just look for the nearest shoe store and figure that it was meant to be.

So when a male hummingbird recently refused to leave after a hard freeze took the flowers, I was immediately alarmed. It was certainly lost and didn't realize that it should be heading to the Southern Hemisphere for the winter.

As I chipped the ice in the feeder, the hummer waited patiently nearby. I could easily tell that it was a male because he had an identifying brilliant ruby coat, common to the Midwest. He was also belching and scratching himself. While he read "Girly Bird Magazine," I quickly cooked his nectar to the requested medium rare.

I couldn't help but develop a liking for the poor lost thing and gave daily email reports that, yes, it was still here. When snow flakes swirled around, however, I knew that it was in dire straits. I tried to furnish maps and calendars to the feeder each day, but to no avail.

So I finally announced to the work boss that I would be gone for a few days because I had to drive a vagrant hummingbird to Central America. He rolled his eyes, but was used to my hag-shenanigans. It seems that I had no vacation time left since the last stint when I needed the day to repair my knitting that one of my cats ruined.

My next ploy to save the map-less male hummer was to run out and buy a cage to hang in the kitchen with feeder inside. It would have a winter's supply of "Girly Bird Magazine" and its own remote control for the Gaggle Network. Not only that, but this hummer's winter digs would feature an easy-street life when it would send out the kitchen hag to make a living with an Audubon Society-approved home and veterinarian medical benefits.

But a friend reminded me that hummingbirds are such a protected bird in the environment that I would be in violation. The Audubon Society would promptly arrest me for depriving a bird from its natural environment.

I envisioned explaining to the AS that this hummer was a vagrant male and that it refused to ask directions. That would save me from being arrested, especially as they would ask me if it scratched, belched and watched Super Gaggle Sunday. The AS would then do a home search of my house to make sure that it was appropriate for a winter's environment.

That should be no problem, since the hummingbirds during the summer season staked out my house as THE place to gather with an endless supply of sugar nectar. They elbowed each other and talked slick hummer slang about the hag's house on the block with an occasional wine vintage and bar stools on the feeder reservoir.

"What's on tap today?" one hummer flitted past another, "Sugar Chardonnay with a twist of ants. She doesn't close at sundown and I hear that she serves during the winter, also. I'll meet you there."
And one imbiber still feeds. He's the one who refuses to ask directions because he has it too good here.

# A New and Improved Hag-zi Scheme

I had a friend define a Ponzi scheme for me the other day. It's not that I am that ignorant about investments or anything, but the last time I opened my checkbook, moths flew out and flapped around my head. They laughed themselves silly when I inquired about perhaps investing something.

There really was a guy by the name of Ponzi, so I am informed, who infamously pulled off a scheme early in the 20th century that made robbing Peter to pay Paul look like a lemonade stand business.

When I looked up the guy, I was already lost about terms that define investment schemes. I had heard of a pyramid deal, fraud and the get-rich-quick stuff, but Matrix, Slatkin and double shah? My favorite is the currently coined word, "Ponzimonium." I was probably dizzy with the swirling checkbook moths laughing at me.

The way I see it, the fraudulent schemers are nothing more than fast-talking charmers that speak from the side of their mouths and entice people looking for those elusive dollar signs. I guess they never recited the Golden Rule with their grandmothers.

I pretended for just a minute the other day how I would organize my own hag-zi scheme. This is, of course, assuming that I understand anything about investments to begin with. So let's say that I collect pizza money from my hag friends on a Sunday evening when we are unfit to be seen in public restaurants. "But," I entice, "if you throw in an extra dollar, I will invest it in anti-wrinkle creams at a rate return of 150 percent."

I don't know how I came up with the high rate of return, but it sounded good coming out of the side of my mouth. Hag friends are always looking for ways to make more money over and above Social Security, short of murdering ex-husbands.

"Hey, sign me up!" they chorus and assume that they will be richer and younger looking. So then I take the extra dollars and instead buy dark chocolate. But never mind that, I've already invited other hag friends for pizza and anti-wrinkle investments. Pretty soon, my fast hag-talking spreads around town with the money-making pizza party scheme.

Meantime, I also print up some most official appearing stationary that says "Hag Enterprises." The ink is black, the font is dead serious and I am rolling in chocolate. Each new pizza event brings in more hag funds and soon I would be on top of a "robbing Pollyanna to pay Paulette" scheme.

Then I had to work on the slick fast-talking image. No longer could I just sit around in my jogging pants, oversized tees or scuff-abouts. I upgraded my wardrobe now that the money was rolling in every time I invited hags to order pizza.

Oh sure, I would print out phony reports on the anti-wrinkle cream business with testimonials about how it is possible to look 20 years younger without getting rid of your husband and teenagers.

Sometimes, I would actually pay out 150 percent return, but only to those who supported my effort to lie around on the couch from day to day and just knit and watch murder movies. The rest of the investors sent the money and as long as I wrote thank-you notes with flowers and lipstick, all was great.

Sometimes, I would hold actual stockholders meetings. I don't know what stockholders do at them; I guess count money that doesn't exist. I noticed, however, that the glares were increasing, I was getter fatter and had nothing intelligent to say except that I had forgotten the Golden Rule.

# The Face of Hagbook

**B**etween tweets, blobs and mugbook computer accounts, there is something new in cyberspace at every keystroke. I used to just humdrum check my email, but that is passé login activity now. Now, you have to have at least a dozen ways to stay in touch with someone that lives in the same town. Or that you saw five minutes ago.

If I contact a friend, I first login yet another password in my growing collection, then type, "How R U?" My message goes from my house across the country to the host site, hop-scotches in space with some satellites, circles the moon a few times, then arrives at my friend's house six blocks away. With little time for cyber-lag, she keys in her response, "I'm OK."

We used to pick up a landline (landline: an archaic method of communication that requires physical wires and an unwieldy apparatus to hold at one's ear) to accomplish the same thing.

Hey, it's a new age now, so I'll just go with it. But with all this hop-scotching around satellites and circling the moon, the new and improved communications still are not communicating anything worth reading (reading: the act of looking at words to make sense of and learn). I enjoy following some tweets that put out something interesting to think about, or a Facebook muse about a worldly event. Much of the time, however, there are chronicles about what time the hiccups started and when they went away. Or how many times a day that one goes to the bathroom.

So I just might start my own spinoff site called "Hagbook." To qualify, your photo must clearly suggest that you have several chins, gray hair and bifocals. But, all is forgiven if you can't get your photo onto the site because there are too many pixels around your midriff.

To sign up, the first thing that you must agree to is that you have read a book or two in recent history (book: an object that you hold in your hands and turn pages to read correctly spelled words in complete sentences).

The idea about reading a book is to determine that you still know how to perceive the English language (English language: a rapidly vanishing form of communication).

You must also agree that you have no idea how to load a video clip onto your Hagbook site (video clip: live documentation of your arms flapping while wielding the salt shaker and when your stomach jiggles every time you laugh).

Very little else is required to sign up, except perhaps your birth date, unless you don't want additional spam-vertisements about mortuaries. If you want to screen out those pesky unwanted ads for anti-wrinkle creams and incontinence products (incontinence: a condition that requires you to install a bathroom nearer to the back door), have a shield that says to verify "Ugly Hag" for incoming messages.

So armed with your little page of brilliance, you reach out to your hagbook friends and put out some profound ideas (profound: thoughtful as in seeing the bigger picture instead of worrying about hiccups) from day to day like, "To be, or not to be." And you wait for some brilliant responses.

But there are none because your hagbook friends are too busy trying to remember their passwords. Finally, an "Is you is, or is you ain't?" comes back. Oh, I forgot. That friend has Alzheimer's and cannot decipher between Shakespeare and Cab Calloway.

So welcome to Hagbook and together, we'll rewrite history (history: when people just talked to each other face to face).

# A Gorilla-Sized Hot Flash, Probably

I read a deadpan newspaper article recently about some gorilla research at several zoos. It seems that it began with an aging female gorilla, Alpha, that was experiencing symptoms of menopause. The observation prompted further study to see if indeed species other than humans experience outliving fertile years with a change of life.

There were hormone levels to check, blood tests to administer and probably behavioral studies to reveal any sign of hostility when male gorillas enter the cage.

The photograph accompanying the article eerily resembled mine when surrounded by family at the Christmas dinner table. Alpha was prune-faced, weighted with jowls and had a generally sour expression about her. The researchers didn't mention it, but Alpha probably overate chocolate and drank expensive wine. Her stomach was bulging and there were probably varicose veins, though the photograph didn't show such. She had graying hair as she glared at her mate, or ex-mate as the case might be.

Her zoo mate, Ramar, had been refusing advances these days. The article said that he was "rather more interested in younger females." Alpha would strut about and throw hay in his face while he barely noticed.

That photograph looked eerily like my marriage portrait. Alpha gestured in her most beautiful stance while Ramar propped his head and rolled his eyes. A curvy blond gorilla likely minced by.

After a series of grunts that displayed an argument about jealousy, Alpha probably communicated a question like, "Do I look fat after eating bananas?" But alas, there was no response since zoo research also probably indicates that males watching Super Gorilla Sunday are declared legally deaf.

21

Or when she lovingly groomed him, he turned away, probably dreaming about a blond gorilla with silky hair and swishing rear end.

But Alpha has her entertainment, also, especially Lifetime movies where the female gorillas murder the male gorillas. Or perhaps the stories where handsome younger gorillas take a fancy to older female gorillas, sweep them off their knuckles and swing off into the vines.

The research is ongoing, but the probable result might indicate that menopausal gorillas might find a better lifestyle. She will probably have a well-stocked pantry of exotic bananas and other various desirable leafy menus. She will probably seek her own quarters where she can sleep in peace and quiet without the male gorilla belching, snoring and nose honking.

The female will probably gather with her like-menopausal friends and gossip about those two-timing zoo mates that tell her when to clean her banana peels and control her every move. They will laugh about all those knuckle-dragging stories when the zoo arrested their mates for disturbing the peace, public consumption of fermented bananas and generally looking disheveled around perfectly respectable, upstanding pillars of the gorilla community.

The best part of research will probably be that menopausal female gorillas will end up more intelligent than their mates or ex-mates still scratching themselves.

Probably.

# A Grandmother's Folly

It is likely that Robert Fulton did not invite any goofy grandmothers aboard when he launched his Clermont. The Fulton's Folly of early 19th century made it 150 miles from New York to Albany without incident. Or without goofy grandmothers powered by 5-year old-grandsons.

A recent visit with my grandson began ordinarily at the park where there were things to climb and a merry-go-round to get dizzy from. My only job was to wave 36 times from a bench as the gleeful smile appeared and disappeared.

But then he noticed that there were these ducks, "but they aren't real," he emphasized. I told him that the real geese were plentiful and we would have a pleasant time watching them tend their gaggle. "Let's just go over here."

"No!" I was wrong and had to follow him the other way at breakneck speed to the riverside. Indeed, the ducks weren't real. They seemed to be a form of river transportation, and I was immediately drafted into being an AARP captain-ess of a big duck. It had two pedals and seemed a bit leaky.

I had driven a lot of vehicles in my life including cars, pickups and a forklift or two. But I had never powered a six-foot yellow duck. There was also a purple dragon, but my grandson had already done a swan dive onto the first duck he saw.

I had to quickly recall my earlier days of stepping onto a floating thing. I had forgotten how the entire body of water shifts while the boat bobs the opposite direction. I was once thrown into a pool by a sly male who thought that my purse should get wet. I laughed about that for a long time. I am also on record for diving off of bridges into some swimming hole. I thought nothing of water slides. My floating repertoire includes boats, canoes, docks and rafts.

But now there was no time to remember that I was less steady than I used to be. He was jacketed, in place and ready to go. I was still getting my varicose land legs adjusted to river legs with the help of the yellow duck guy. In earlier times, I didn't mind a misstep or two, splash, oh whoops, I guess I'm wet. I also didn't mind wearing a bathing suit in public then.

So here I was, perched in a yellow duck and looking to stay dry with purse and cell phone in tow. And the side-seat-driver five-year-old.

Right away, my side began sinking. The duck must be engineered incorrectly, I convinced myself. In order to balance ourselves and stay afloat, I moved to the center, trying not to look like Big Bird on a big duck. But then there were the bicycle pedals that I couldn't reach from that position.

"Grandma!" he squealed that we were too close to the edge.

"Grandma!" he squealed that we were going in circles.

By then I worried about the riverbank filling with an audience waiting either to come to the aid of a duck's folly, or be entertained by a grandmother folly. I could see the local headlines; "Grandmother drowns, five-year-old pedals to the Mississippi." Or, "Yellow duck capsizes, five-year-old saves the day."

I had no time to look for potential crowds, however, because I was obviously still trying to learn the steering mechanism, pedal sideways, keep the squeals satisfied and hope that my cell phone speed dial stayed dry.

By the time we pedaled our way back, my grandson was just getting started on adventure and I was finished. Next time I'll look for an ocean liner with deck chairs to sit on and wave from.

# A Resolution For Jack Sprat

He's the one who could eat no fat, while his wife could eat no lean.

I can't put my finger on how the rest of the rhyme went, but I think that she died happily and he remarried into a dysfunctional family that refused to speak at the wedding reception because he wouldn't go off his diet long enough to eat chocolate wedding cake. I think.

Then Sprat found that his new wife had a closet addiction to Reese's peanut butter clusters and, after a few months of marital discord, began gaining weight rapidly. Not only that, but she had lied about her ability to cook lean and presented him with frozen dinners that included potatoes, gravy and butter-sauced everything. I think.

The new Mrs. Sprat was also an insatiable collector of salt shakers. Not just any old salt shakers, but ones filled with salt. She developed an inordinate passion for throwing salt over her left shoulder, hitting Sprat in the face and bringing tears to his eyes. But the tears were really about his second dysfunctional marriage. I think.

She was also a shopaholic, knitaholic, lousy housekeeper ya da ya da ya da.

So Sprat filed for divorce to rid himself of wives with excesses unacceptable in his predictable no-fat life. He learned his lesson about marriage and died a lonely man. I think.

So much for people out there who seem to have no bad habits. They are boring and leave no legacy of character or goofy stories. They never make it beyond a simple rhyme.

When you think about historical figures, there have been no accomplished men who are like Jack Sprat. No President Sprat, King Sprat, or Secretary of State Jack Sprat. He was never Mohammad Spratli,

Hollywood heartthrob Paul Spratman or remembered in darker history as Jack the Spratter or Adolph Spratler. A guy by the name of Sprat never conquered countries, wrote classic novels or anointed himself man-of-the hour for dressing slick and being a ladies man. He never once bragged about his feats on the football field, mainly because he'd never been there.

He was simply sitting straight at the table with folded hands and saying, "no thank you" to life's excesses.

He says, "no thank you" to everything. He probably never went to a bar and said stupid things. He probably never bought a polka dot tie or a brightly colored tee shirt. He probably never threw his leg over the arm of a chair and cussed at life in general. He probably never used a credit card to buy something frivolous. In fact, he probably only bought lean meat and lettuce.

I am thankful to have no Jack Sprats in my immediate circle of friends and family (the family that still speaks). I'd rather surround myself with flawed and flamboyant people with excesses galore. My love goes out to those who can't stop at just one cookie or have to sneak an expensive purchase past a suspicious spouse. I love those that hide chocolate kisses behind the drapes or brandy behind the clothes dryer. I love those who shake at the sight of jewelry stores.

And there are always the non-Sprats who make bad decisions in life. One of my favorite acquaintances conveniently forgot about upcoming dental work and purchased an expensive piece of artwork. She could have been the third Mrs. Sprat, but turned down his advances because he was simply too boring. Or maybe he had already died lonely.

So, if your name is Jack Sprat, my advice is, lighten up.

# A Seismic Event

To most of us, the word "seismic" would refer to some major news story about California falling into its old fault line habit of jiggling the West Coast for a terrifying period of time.

The San Andreas Fault is not the only culprit for a seismic event. The Midwest has had a jiggle or two and threatens many more with its own sleeping fault underneath our feet. One awoke me in the middle of the night about five years ago when the window pane sounded like a giant stomping through villages clenching his fist to find hags with 100 percent cotton floral pajamas. The entire countryside said, "ahem," he disappeared and we all went back to sleep.

My daughter never felt anything, of course, because she overslept her entire high school. An earthquake would have to lift her mattress and deposit her into an urn of freshly-brewed coffee before she would even notice anything awry. "Mom? What was that noise? Did you trip over your knitting?"

But the word "seismic" applies to other facets about our lives that require a steady hand with a handy shot of whiskey for medicinal purposes. I once had a friendly mailman hand deliver a full color photograph of my car speeding through a construction zone. One mile over the limit, and some magic camera dangles from the fist of that giant stomping through Interstates.

I told the judge that there were no workers present, but "Well, ma'am," he thundered and I consequently shook enough to cause the Bailiff to steady herself as he handed down a million dollar fee, "payable through that door." That was a seismic event when I donated blood and organs to pay off the ticket.

The same Interstate giant hovered in the I-pass lane soon after. It hid warning signs and re-arranged huge trucks so that I was blinded toward the pay lane. The same photograph with the same mailman arrived with a handy bill to cover the rest of the State deficit for the year 2009.

That seismic reaction shook the foundation of my house. I flopped onto the couch with such a heavy sigh that a new fault line, "San Andreas Hag" was born underneath my basement. It hovers quietly most of time, but becomes active only when official State mail arrives. Or when a daughter sends a stormy email about everything that she knows, and nothing that I know.

My ex-husband used to enter the room as his own seismic event. Noticing some genetic similarity, my son stomps through a room heavy enough to awaken the "San Andreas Hag" underneath the basement. I once laid some new parquet flooring for him to notice, but he was too focused on walking over it toward the bathroom. "What new flooring?" The one that cost hundreds of dollars and lots of labor!

So, I recently visited a friend's ex-husband for a new round of laughs and noticed that his kitchen clock didn't move for more than two hours. Well, he's a busy man so maybe overlooked a dead battery. I thought that I would help out and teetered on a chair to ask for the correct battery.

No, he deadpanned that a "seismic event" caused the demise of the clock. It wasn't the Interstate giant or the free lane giant or the San Andreas Hag fault that keeps the State budget healthy. It was rather a tradesman hammering on the roof of the house to cause the clock to fly off the wall.

I am glad that he cleared that up.

# A Leggy Situation

There is a saying that you are never more than three feet away from a spider. If I had never heard that, I might be sleeping better for the rest of my life.

As ignorance is bliss, I must have been happy-go-lucky before that spider warning to think that I could simply put clean, airy sheets and fresh pillow cases on my bed and fall asleep. Sweet dreams with no spiders staring at me. And that my house was leg-free with no sneaky roommates that wait for me to sleep and have their way with the walls and corners.

But now I am thinking that the room might have 84 legs waiting to attack old hags wearing 100 percent cotton. Oops, according to my calculator, that includes a half spider. OK, so 88 legs.

So now, I am thrust into a situation where I am always on guard for those creepy legs nearby. I am told that we only see females because she destroys the male after mating, thereby eliminating the expensive and drawn out divorce proceedings once the male messes up the web with his eight smelly socks.

Or maybe her mate has a wandering eye for the neighboring web where the female has shapelier legs and moves with svelte grace in a ballet tutu. I don't know, do spiders have eye lashes? And if they socially dance, how many left feet are there?

So I was minding my own business with my crossword puzzle before me the other night. This follows a day when I tackled a few things in the basement and swept down some cobwebs in the process. I knew that my basement had a few webs here and there, but I thought that they all lived in marital bliss, or murderous mating, in the basement. I made a pact; you keep your legs down there and I'll keep my legs up here. Ne'er the twain shall meet.

Staring at my puzzle, I couldn't help but notice out of the corner of my eye a fat spider making its way across the room toward me. What caught my attention is that she was wearing eight mesh stockings in loud colors and designer Stiletto heels. She was also hefty and mad looking.

She was not heading for the kitchen, or a dark corner or a nice dank basement via furnace outlet. She was heading for me and in a hurry! I'm sure that she had had a bad day what with a recognizable hag who came along to destroy her happy home. She had just killed her mate for leaving his clumpy shoes around. Murder is pretty stressful, after all, to a feminine spider trying to be a single parent to family of eggs.

At that moment of ambush, I wondered where my attack-anything-that-moves cat was. His name is "Tripod," with only three legs. No shoes, no fancy pants, just three legs poised for action. He is by no means handicapped, but has a habit of napping when I need him the most.

So my only defense at that moment was my own two legs wearing sweat pants and a crossword puzzle weapon. Me against her; she goes. Thwap! Gone were the mesh tights in neon colors and Stiletto high heels.

By the time I recovered my presence of mind and found a new puzzle without road kill, I determined that I probably need to assess the spider situation. It is too many legs to suit my taste. Now, my next worry is if I destroy all those happy and murderous homes in the basement, they will all come after me at once.

# A Standardized Landfill

It's no wonder that our landfills are filling fast. I actually haven't visited one, though I might include it on my vacation list if my budget doesn't improve.

I am suspicious that our landfills are simply last week's cell phone parts. If you want to know what next week's landfill material is, go to the store. Any store. Cruise the aisles with all the bubble wraps, ten digit part numbers with a backwards letter thrown in here and there and a laundry list of what each is compatible with. Nothing. And to think that I took out my most powerful reading glasses to discover that.

What ever happened to the 19th century and that miraculous revolution when parts became standardized? I think I remember studying about it in high school. It was considered a novelty to have parts to interchange all over instead of having the local blacksmith, or local whoever, bang out a custom replacement.

So the blacksmith or local whoever has been replaced by an entire continent on the other side of the planet that sends us sizes of parts that don't fit unless we spend new money for something that we already have. It seems that the right hand should talk to the left hand. But that would make too much sense.

No, I don't want to return to horse and buggies, outhouses and the days before we understood cooties and cleanliness. I just want my upgraded cell phone to fit my last five attachments. I am on my third car jack and second set of ear phones. Actually, I accidentally left one wall jack on a vacation last year. This year, when I stay at the Landfill Inn, I'll remember to pack everything. While touring the scenic landfill, I'll probably find what I need, anyway, one week old that someone else had to discard.

33

Yes, I could be advised by some stick-in-the-muds against needing a cell phone to begin with. And no, I don't text or talk while driving or have to call a friend every five minutes to ask if her hair has grown any since the last call. If a constant, "What are you doing?" in life is all there is everyday, then it's no wonder no one is employed; everyone's on the cell phone asking dumb questions.

I love my cell, however, for road emergencies or boogey men with a fetish for hags with chins lurking around the corner. It's most handy at the store when having a sudden Alzheimer's episode. "What was I supposed to get again?" Oh, that's right, wine, chocolate and roses. The basics.

One might think that ear phones are extraneous toys with a cell phone, but just try to balance a wafer thin thing between your ear and shoulder while doing important things like making coffee. Then you have to visit the chiropractor or, worse yet, retrieve the cell phone from the flushing toilet. Our old landline phone, humungous by description, at least fit neatly so we could use both hands.

Those handy dandy days are gone, now, along with standardized parts that fit. I have tried to defy the system by jerry-rigging the prongs. jerry-rigging, of course, is something that we all have to do occasionally to make things work. Duct tape is standard.

But, to no avail. There were 17 prongs on a trapezoid-shaped plug that wouldn't fit into 15 prongs on a triangle. The two were as incompatible as oil and water or ex-husbands in current households of hags that glare.

If anyone needs me, I'll be touring the landfill.

# A Wolf in Sheep's Clothing

It's my Halloween costume this year. I figure if major corporations and politicians can put on a false front to speak to the herd, then I can too.

I thought of this the other day when I was trying to decide what costume to wear to a Halloween party. I am tired of the regular masquerades that include bell bottoms and peace signs from the '60s, pigs with lipstick and ballet tutus designed for hags with varicose veins.

I'll just don a three-piece suit and carry around a podium.

My opening remarks over the podium will be inspired by a real life CEO that I listened to about five years ago (honest 'injun):

A major corporation was trying to quell employee fears that their particular facility would close and move operations out of the country. It seemed like the trend at the time, and the newest big shot couldn't wait to rub his palms and salivate at the bottom line on the screen. So this particular big shot brought in a new CEO to make a speech.

He was wearing sheep's clothing.

The speech began with a mild-mannered, "I don't like ships because they sink." He had a convincing demeanor about him that was supposed to assure the workers that if he didn't like ships that, oh gosh, "therefore this facility was not moving overseas to have its product travel over scary waters with carnivorous sharks that manufacture American products and, therefore, you loyal workers need not fear because I am the only CEO to keep manufacturing on the shores of these United States."

They got rid of that CEO before he took questions from the floor. The CEO in sheep's clothing was basically hired to make a rubber-ducky bathtub speech.

Another CEO, also wearing sheep's clothing, claimed that the sale of

35

this particular facility to another company had nothing to do with operations moving overseas but rather that all domestic workers would benefit from great profits, pensions and a lifetime supply of chocolate. "It's a win-win situation," said the wolf in sheep's clothing. That facility became a wart of cement on the landscape almost overnight.

So with my three-piece suit and traveling podium, I'll say, "trick or treat," then give speeches about how wonderful I am. I will go into accolades about how honorable and forthright my ideas about a perfect life and that my house is perfectly clean.

I'll go on to claim that I am always sweet with kind thoughts so that everyone loves to hear what I have to say. Why the other day, I would orate, everyone in the work place cheered because I vowed to be a perfect example of company dedication. My co-workers clamored to agree that I was a perfect employee who always followed every rule with loyal subservience. Why, I never do crossword puzzles on company time, nor return from breaks 30 seconds later than approved.

With sheep's clothing and my podium, I'll go on about being a worker who never smart-mouths bosses or co-workers that pretend they are important supervisors.

On the home front, my house is always clean, my laundry always put away and checkbook always in order. There are no pesky pet hairs anywhere or dust bunnies that you can invite to dinner.

I never drink wine or eat chocolate while no one is looking. There are no kernels of popcorn in my car or gum wrappers under the seat.

I exercise religiously everyday of my whole life and do jumping jacks at the mere thought of fast food.

It's the most fun Halloween costume I've ever worn!

# ANtS iN My PaNtS

Come spring and summer, there might be an invasion in our perfectly civilized houses. I noticed that last week when various things with creepy legs seemed to like my kitchen.

About various creepy legs, I've seen a centipede or two with a limousine of appendages rush across the room directly above the basement. With all its legs, it didn't seem to make it past the bottom of my shoe. Then I would spend the next ten minutes horrified and wondering how I would survive with only two legs against a hundred.

Cockroaches, of course, are great fun to tell wild stories about at a party. There are fish tales about exactly how big they are and always some college reference to one enterprising cockroach strong enough to carry away a roommate's shoe.

Long ago in my wilder years, I had a friend stay with me for a stint. I knew that she had cockroaches in her previous apartment, so we carefully cleaned each object on the front porch before it came inside. Never mind that, the roach population simply marched through the back door and had already set up housekeeping by the time we came in. They were relaxing on the couch and had bedroom communities between the walls.

I sterilized a lot, but in the end Mr. Roachgetter had to rid me of those creepy things along with that "friend." And I am itchy with ants in my pants just thinking about it.

So then here comes some goofy ant moseying across the kitchen floor the other day. It wasn't that he was lost because he seemed to be carrying a steamer trunk of belongings. He also had that look about him that said willful intent about moving in. Then I saw him wave in the rest of the family but, too late, he expired underneath my shoe.

The next morning, the family of the fallen ant marched in a parade including a pampered queen escorted by her court, some low life workers and a glaring mother-in-law. They were all carrying suitcases. My shoe traveled around the kitchen with murder in mind. Some never knew what hit them, and others went slowly. I think I heard an, "Oh woe is me!" somewhere. The pampered queen, however, set up her throne out of sight.

Then I knew that I had better arm myself with ant traps, the kind that are out of sight from lazy cats that drape around on chairs. The skull-and-crossbones ant-getter went under the sink. I stood back in a warlike stance, daring any self-respecting ant to cross my path.

The directions said that the ants would poison themselves, then return to their pampered queen to conspire to murder her. By the time a friend came over, I was slapping my shoe in the dining room at what seemed a bigger invasion – more parades, more suitcases and more glaring mothers-in-law.

Every time I sat down to talk to the friend, something black carrying a suitcase would move across the dining room floor. But then, I thought, maybe they're not carrying suitcases, but rather in a dither at the loss of their pampered queen. Yeah, that's it. They're grieving about a tragic situation and preparing to leave. I hoped.

Then the next day, I was sitting on the back porch admiring my hummingbird feeder filled with fresh and enticing sugar water. The hummers came and went, but a closer look was that ants had crawled in to commit suicide in the feeder. They were the same ants with suitcases. Not too sharp.

But I still get itchy with ants in my pants.

# Abetting the Rumor Mill

It churns day in and day out by the internet, media and just plain people talking over the fence or at the water cooler.

The work place is a favorite for rumor action these days. The stories are more like tavern talk where you learn to shrug and dismiss the bragging and scandals. You can't help but be amused meantime.

My true story is that I once took a vacation day to fatten a weekend. My luck turned south with a nasty flu bug that put me under the weather. I called in for two more days as I shivered and ached under blankets.

It is a boring story, but life is that way sometimes.

When I returned to work with Kleenex and aspirin in tow, I heard from two sources who heard it from so-and-so that such-and-such person said that I had been sent home for three days due to a "disciplinary" discharge. The story was that I was guilty of an "act of violence" against another employee. And there were so many versions of the story that I was confused about what I actually did. I promise that the above is true.

The more I thought about it, however, the funnier it got. I was really concerned that the story of this alleged violence was rather uncreative. So I thought that I'd help it along…

Oh sure, there was violence, but not at work. When the mailman had the nerve to deliver a credit card bill, I threw a brick at him to set him straight. He escaped without injury, but I was already hatching another plan.

My plan for my credit card bill, I theorized with shifty eyes, got down to two methods; rob a bank or sell my body. Sleuthing both options, I decided, would be a sure thing.

The first day off, though I told no one, I checked into breast augmentation surgery. It was my first in a series of cosmetic upgrades to better my chances to use my body as a marketable tool. Marketable for what, I hadn't decided.

The surgeons, straight out of degree mills through Mother Goose, mistakenly overcompensated the material and left behind several instruments, a shroud and a nurse's cell phone.

Shaped now like a sack of potatoes, I was determined to keep my date with the bank.

I swept in disguised and lipsticked, coolly slipping a note to my favorite teller. "This is a holdup," it said, "give me your cash and don't look at my chest." I was wobbling in Stiletto heels.

Since I never took a course in "Bank Robbery 101," I unwittingly wrote the note on the back of my own deposit slip. When the tellers gathered and noticed my name, they laughed so hard that they forgot to call the police. Dejected, I went home with an overdraft slip.

As luck would have it, I got a call to appear in Siberia the next day to accept a literary prize for writing the most dysfunctional sentence in the most ridiculous column category. I packed my bags quickly, but forgot about my sack-of-potatoes chest that seemed to outsize my prize-accepting wardrobe. No matter, because it wouldn't pass security at the airport. The media showed up to interview the terrorist hag that attempted to board with imbedded scalpels.

How did they get there? was the burning question of the day. I told them that I swallowed circus knives for a living along with a few wine stems. I slipped past the snickering reporters, but the plane was then high-jacked by some cheapskate who...

Thankfully, I was able to return to work safe and sound by Wednesday. It was certainly heart-warming to know that so many work people cared about my weekend.

# AS EaSy aS FaLLiNg OUt oF Bed

G etting out of bed in the morning can be hazardous to your health. I learned this a while back during that path from alarm clock to clean socks.

It began like every other morning. Hum drum. Sit up and contemplate life after the alarm clock. I reached over for socks in the laundry basket. It was one of those weeks when clean clothes didn't quite make it to the dresser drawers. They did make it up from the basement, so I should get a gold star for that.

As I braced myself with one hand on the bed, I reached into the basket with the other. My hand slipped down the side of the bed onto the corner of the frame that happened to have a minuscule burr ready for slicing my arm open. I'm sure that burr said "Bull's Eye," but there was too much blood that distracted me to hear talking furniture. Ouch! I thought, along with some other unladylike words. But life goes on, and I continued to get ready for the day.

It was then that I noticed a trail of blood from bedroom to bathroom. Oh well, a few Band-aids and I'll be on my way. No big deal. The wound was so deep, however, that I was still stuffing paper towels into my jacket sleeve on the way to the emergency room.

You can understand many household accidents that need little explanation. Falling down the stairs, for instance, is on my resume of dumb mishaps around the house. Another infamous event was the wood sliver about the size of a baseball bat that imbedded itself under a fingernail. After minor surgery and turning all colors of the rainbow, including yellow and green, the nail simply ballooned and gave birth to the sliver on its own.

There are other honorable mishaps. Cutting oneself with a paring knife while slicing onions, or a common bagel stab deserves emergency room respect. A work friend even tore up his knee while on a trampoline with his son.

But falling out of bed would have to be something to be explained. I'm sure that the hospital staff was ready to do a blood-alcohol test. "You did what?" the doctor asked and everyone's ear was cupped to hear the steamy details of an old hag criminal or some spousal abuse.

Five stitches later, he warned that there probably would be a scar. I told him that my bikini days were over, thank you, and that one more set of railroad tracks was nothing to be alarmed about. But he was still asking how I could fall out of bed, like a lawyer toward the witness stand looking for changes in the story. Gradually the truth would come out.

"And then the drug deal went bad," I should have said, "when the guy pulled a knife and threw me against the wall because I was ugly with too many chins and a hanging stomach. Then he demanded my wallet, which had $2, three gasoline receipts, a washer for the kitchen faucet and a prescription for incontinence.

"This enraged him even more," I should have told the inquiring doctor, "so he tried to steal something from my bedroom, but could only find flannel nightgowns, '70s earrings and anti-wrinkle cream on the nightstand. So he went to the refrigerator, but could only find designer water, moldy cheese, a half yogurt and something green in the back. Then he sliced my arm and fled into the night."

I'm sorry, but I just fell out of bed.

# Being the Fool That's Born Every Minute

I'm the one who makes the car salesmen rub their palms together on sight.

It began recently when I realized that I spend more time at the car repair shop than the grocery store. No wonder the mechanics are so friendly showing piano teeth when they smile "Hi" and "Bye" after exchanging life stories. It's because my car single-handedly supports their garage. When it "nickels and dimes you to death," as they say, it's time to look for another car.

A friend was in the same dilemma when her car repeatedly died on the way to work. She became fast friends with the same tow truck guy who always greeted her and asked about the family and how her sister's surgery went the week before.

We agreed that the experience of buying a new car is right up there with a root canal or tax audit.

It's not that I dislike cars or anything, but I've always regarded them as the fast lane to rust and ruin. They soak up your finances with payments, then exactly five minutes after you have paid them off, they faint dead away into car title history. It's the ultimate conspiracy against working slobs who can never get ahead.

So with that cornered feeling of despair, I left the repair shop and thought I'd just casually "browse" at a local car sale. My daughter said, "Oh, mom, it wouldn't hurt to look," thinking that I was probably the most boring person in the world about spur-of-the-moment events. You know, see what's available, run home to the calculator and rearrange my entire budget to exclude designer water and new walking shoes for five years to afford car payments.

Within two minutes of my arrival at the car place, a red carpet rolled out from nowhere followed by a car salesman straight out of "GQ Magazine" and serving cappuccino. With his velvet voice, he said a most friendly, "May I help you?" It was then that I noticed his eyes were just a bit too close together as he winked at fellow salesmen the code phrase, "This sucker's mine."

"Oh, I'm just looking," said the fly to the spider.

Once he shook my hand, a desk magically appeared emitting a seductive new car aroma. "Well, let's find out what you're looking for," he said as a flurry of papers and brochures dropped from the sky.

Well, I'm too slick for salesmen, I thought, so I'll just be impossible to please. The first priority, I told him with an air of hostility, was "I want superior gas mileage, like a couple decades ago when I got 50 miles per gallon on the road." He shuffled his papers, rearranged his tie and whispered something about the oil companies. A point for me.

I went on with my list. "I want a sun roof with handy astrology chart, a five-speed stick so that the young punk thieves can't drive it, an automatic aroma therapy button and velvet-lined trunk to house my groceries and anti-wrinkle creams."

I continued my demands with information about my lack of finances, no money down and low payments. He still didn't flinch, but upped the ante bit by bit without my noticing. When he was satisfied that I had agreed to go on welfare to make car payments, a gaggle of salesmen appeared from nowhere to shake my hand. I was putty in their hands.

The next thing I said was "Quick, where do I sign?"

I was still taking medication for nervous stomach when I called a friend to secretly admit that I love it! Payments and all, but don't tell the salesmen.

# Reaching the Whopper Threshold

One thing that I will miss if I am ever allowed to retire from the workplace is my favorite form of entertainment; people. Not just regular, normal people, but the spectrum of characters that every large organization has in its roster.

There are always the Slackers, of course. They're the ones that everyone has contempt for. The dutiful workers wonder how it is that the Slackers get away with slacking. I was once told by a boss that "We expect so much more from you, Sue." The logical end to that, I pondered, would be to become more of a Slacker. But in the end, I would have no such luck to get away with it.

Also in the end, the Slackers don't get away with it, either, without promotions or even ongoing employment. We had a marvelous version of Ralph Cramden who strutted his stuff around without the slightest inclination to do the job. He regularly slept on his forklift using the propane tank for a pillow. His waking hours at work were spent on his perpetual pre-break breaks. The classic question was "Where is he?" Usually he was outside making sports bets from his cell phone or ordering food.

But, alas, he met his demise and is out there trying to find another job where he can get enough sleep at work.

I am also amused by the slick Pretenders who have landed on this earth as a gift to all women. There is always a Marlboro Man that has a stride pretending to have broad shoulders and the swagger straight out of "GQ Magazine." He fancies himself dust-clad with a rough-and-tough image of wisdom and great knowledge about everything. This type of Marlboro Man is usually 22 years old, skinny and buck-toothed.

And then, of course, there are the Braggarts. They are the most fun because their favorite subject in the world is themselves. The Braggart has a bigger, better and more important story at all times. The Braggart also has a nasty habit of racing to the office to tattletale about someone else in an effort to "look good" as a valued company person.

A few of us and a Braggart had what began as a normal discussion about eye color the other day and who had what in their family. Blue eyes, brown eyes and hazel colors were in the dialogue along with an informative article that someone read about blue eyes becoming less common. Not to be outdone by anything that made sense, this very brown-eyed Dusseldorf offered that his were actually "mood eyes." All other eyes immediately rolled to the ceiling awaiting the whopper. It seems that his eyes turn colors from brown to blue to green according to his mood changes.

"Mine are pink," I added, "because I am a girl." I also offered a handy Brooklyn Bridge to sell.

We all laughed, but Dusseldorf was undaunted as his whoppers got bigger. There were escalating stories about his many women and how difficult it is being so popular and how in order to foot his legal fees for a paternity test that he would hold a big benefit because he had "friends" who would play music yada yada yada.

With each escalating whopper, we laughed, rolled our eyes or squirmed. At some point, however, I reached a whopper threshold when my mouth turned into a flame thrower. It happens sometimes like an out-of-body experience and without warning. I heard myself say something about his intellect being located in some other organ of his body.

He tattled, of course, but the boss didn't seem to think I needed correction.

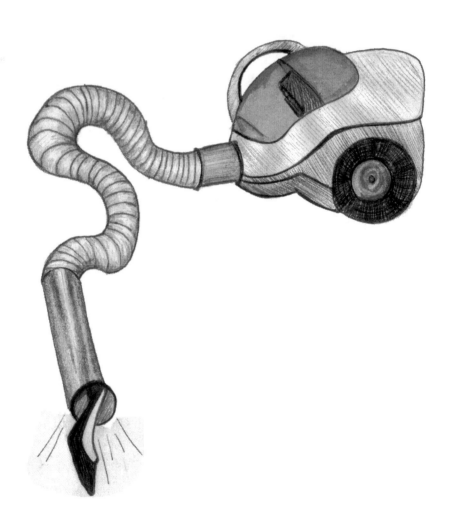

# Accomplishing Great Things
## Up the Suction Hose

I think that we are all capable of accomplishing great things. At least that's what my parents taught me.

Those were the days when axioms, adages and sappy poetry could inspire you to live out your life through rose-colored glasses.

Every day you should appreciate life, they lectured, and do something to improve your mind. Follow your own talent, read something and enjoy each day as if it were you last, they raised a forefinger.

That's if you have time. What they conveniently forgot to include in that happy-thwappy life lecture was that teensy-weensy detail called making a living. Taking care of the business of life these days has nearly sucked up every waking moment as well as every ounce of energy. Then if there's anything left in our brain cells, we might be able to accomplish great things.

Either that, or be independently wealthy and have someone ELSE clean house, grocery shop, do laundry, fill the gas tank, cut the grass…

But nevertheless, I decided that I would take 15 minutes each day to try to accomplish great things. You know, like write a classic American novel, get an advanced degree in nuclear physics, move mountains – little things like that. Saturday was designated Day One for the rest of my life. Fifteen minutes at a time, I told myself, I would live up to my potential. And if all goes well and I live to the age of 146 years old, then I could accomplish great things.

The morning was spent in the car shop – the one that takes my money to get to the job so that I can earn money to pay the car shop.

There was also no coffee in the house. You can't accomplish great things without caffeine. One quick store trip and then I couldn't think straight when I noticed that I was a week behind on my housecleaning.

OK, I'll vacuum and do laundry, then accomplish great things. But the vacuum cleaner was there in the same spot reminding me that it had no suction. A midget-sized dust mite was safe from a hose that lay there dead. Several trips to the store later for the right size filter, and I was disassembling the thing. With new filters in, vacuuming would be a snap, I thought.

Still no suction. The front room turned into a suction hose workshop. There were implements to examine the stomachs of snakes for contraband, Phillip's head screwdrivers of every size except the one I needed and four-letter words that echoed through the hose.

I even recalled my ex-husband who bragged that his vacuum cleaner was from Germany and cost a zillion dollars. It sucks great, he beamed. He even boasted that he could vacuum without bending over to pick up things by hand. His was so advanced and allergen free that he could clean the whole house without once blowing his nose.

Then, heh heh, I ran across another filter that I had overlooked for the five years that I had owned the vacuum. It said "Change every three months, you dummy." It left yet a new trail of dust bunnies to the trash. The new roaring suction was so great that it nearly sucked up the dining room shears. Then the belt broke. Another trip to the store.

By then, it was late afternoon and I had not spent my allocated 15 minutes.

Sometimes, you have to accept the fact that accomplishing great things means that the car oil is changed and the vacuum cleaner hose sucks.

# Calling All Humans

The population stats say that the earth has begat about a jillion human beings these days. And further predictions hike up more people than resources can provide for.

If you're stuck in traffic or stand in a bank line, you can appreciate what overpopulation does to our patience. But pick up the phone, and all bets are off. There is not a human out there from here to the moon.

I tried it the other day to call for service information about my internet/landline/cable bill, and I do use the word "service" with a saw-toothed vibrato in my voice. By the time I shouted "yes" and "no" a few times and punched in a few routing numbers, my hair had turned white and another chin fell. To say nothing about running out of available time in my working life to shout at recordings.

And then when you finally get that live human, your nerves are such on edge that you cannot possibly conduct a lucid communication. My language got so blue once from my cell phone that a tower outside town melted down. It was in response to an internet bill from a service that I had long since changed. The return service was the Wizard of Oz, and there were no humans there, either, to hear out my wrath.

When I finally got a live person about my current problem the other day, I tried to explain to her that I had an extra land line that just served the computer. I wanted to get rid of that line. "It has a different number," I patiently explained, "it could belong to the person next door or someone in Siberia."

She was cheerful enough, spoke English, but didn't get it. I then went into the background of my telephone lines with a little Pony Express information thrown in just for a little historical perspective. She was really lost then since she was probably hatched out of an IPod.

She finally got it when I told her that a live human – that is one with arms, legs, basic knowledge of phone lines and one that the corporation does not want to pay or cover medical benefits for – would have to actually show up at my house and rewire.

I would then answer the door and have a live conversation with this human – a dialogue that requires no recordings, beeps or punching numbers.

So, I figure if "you can't beat'em, join'em," or as Nelson Mandela's wisdom instructs, "learn about your enemy." Why lie down and be a victim just waiting for the next tantrum when you can't find a human being anywhere?

I decided that my answering machine would be my personal firewall against all those non-humans. My greeting will waste everyone else's time, also:

"Hello, you have reached thewritehag of the 'Hot Flashes' column. Please listen carefully to your menu options. If you hate this week's column, press ONE. If you want to run it, anyway, press TWO and just send the check. If you are a bill collector, solicitor or obnoxious recording about giving to any cause other than my own Titanic finances, stay on the line so that I can reach through the phone and strangle your snaky neck. If you are a friend, I'm probably here but refuse to answer the phone because I am in recovery from the last phone call.

"If you are a friend bringing an expensive bottle of wine—Oh, ah Hello! Come right over!" It's always a pleasure to talk to a human.

# Chariot Race Moments of Today

The history books seem to sit there and gather dust, while we repeat the mistakes in their pages. We tend to view all past eras as development into the current Third Age. Then, they were wrong; now, we are right. That's the part of history that repeats itself.

It just depends on when you were born. My mother, for instance, always thought that communism in the Soviet Union was a permanent idea for "those foreigners over there." The history books, however, will hardly acknowledge the social structure's existence in the long run. After all, a mere 70 years is hardly a blip on the historical screen.

My mother also thought, using her '40s college degree in history, that key figures of the past wore either white hats or black hats. Washington, Lincoln and the like wore white hats. Anyone else who didn't refuse to lie about chopping down the cherry tree wore black hats.

I hope that we have learned a little more about history and human nature since then.

I notice that there were blood and gore, for instance, in ancient Rome when arenas filled with thrill-seeking crowds. At least that's what we learned in high school history books. The crowd roared to a fever pitch at every hazard, according to "Ben Hur," the qualifying official history lesson about chariot races. There was even more emotional fervor in that latter history lesson because there were cute guys in the race.

"How low class those Ancients were," my mother would say, "blood-thirsting animals," she distasted. We learned and cultured people of the 21st century could never appreciate such carnivorous entertainment.

But those Ancients are still around. Not just at NASCAR or Indy 500. They are very present on the aggressive and murderous interstate highways. The blood-lusting crowd that gathers to seek thrills and entertainment has a new name. It's called the Gaper's Block.

We continue to be so fascinated with the misfortunes of someone else that we create the world's largest bottleneck to take it in. (The word "bottleneck," by the way, was probably coined by Chicago traffic-flow engineers, an infamous bunch of hopeless alcoholics that designed the merge lane into the fast lane. You do the visuals.)

If the Gaper's Block and the world's largest bottleneck turn out to be a mere fender-bender with two disgruntled drivers on their cell phones calling insurance agents, we are deeply disappointed. We could have bragged for days about being witnesses to an unspeakable scene of carnage.

It would have been our chariot race moment of the day.

I once came across such a scene moments after it happened. There was an upside-down car in the ditch and a shaken elderly driver whose van was totaled. I whipped into high-adrenaline gear.

Two young guys were wandering around the highway, dazed and confused. One asked me where we were and what day it was. I just assured him that he would be fine, but he was too much in shock to hear my answer. The real hero was the lady who witnessed the accident and calmed the driver stuck in the ditch. She urged him not to move and stay awake until help arrived.

I was secretly glad that my car was blocked by emergency vehicles. I wanted so much to be a part of the help action. I wanted to take orders, comfort the injured and wear a Clara Barton nurse's uniform.

I still pass that section on the road and relive that scene. I think that I'm just like every other human being in history who worries about the cute guy in a chariot race.

# Following the Yellow Brick Road

A friend was giving me directions to an event the other day when I suddenly realized that none of it made sense. I was getting more irritable as my notes were filled with arrows, visual cues and which McDonald's to pass.

All I needed was the name of the road and which way to turn. It was only 40 miles away and, last time I checked, east, west, north and south were my only options.

But that would be too easy. After that, I decided that giving directions is a highly interpretive art form that reflects the personality of each person.

For a mechanic, for instance, there are no forks or Y's in the road. "Then there's a crescent wrench-shaped curve next to the power station on the opposite side of a road where there's a cog in the middle," my mechanic friend said.

When my ex-husband gives directions, he begins with "it's easy, you just..." and then waves his arms around pointing in every direction at once. When the whole room spins and everyone gets dizzy, he corrects himself and says, "but then if you go that way, there are too many traffic lights.

I might have known. One time, some friends and I piled into his car to go to a favorite Chicago restaurant. He headed west first, then south, then east. Even friends unfamiliar with Chicago knew that we were driving a buzzard's route to the prey. I dared not ask why, however, because I knew that he would drive ten miles in the opposite direction to avoid one traffic light.

Another version of his directions is the one that gives you the alley route of the entire Chicago metropolitan area. This one avoids traffic cops, allows you to speed and promises no stop signs. The only problem arises when the smirking garbage man clogs your way and makes you go in reverse for about three blocks.

Some give directions without the slightest knowledge of the basic compass. "You turn this way (hold thumb like a hitchhiker), then that way (stand like a safety patrol), then you take this curve (turn into swimming diver). North points toward the ceiling.

Others give you driver's education with directions. "Then you get in the right lane, but slow down first. When the light changes, head for such-and-such street and put your blinker on at the next intersection."

And, of course, the visually explicit. "After you pass that blue house with the cow-shaped mail box, you go until you get to the farm with a round barn, then turn right at the vegetable stand..."

I had a relative who actually got lost in her own directions. Then she would digress into the history of everything. "And so, turn left, or wait a minute, we turned left and had a flat tire. Let's see, was that on Tuesday? No, the milkman comes on Tuesday..."

I then turned to the internet for directions. The first one I came upon had "Welcome, to those lost with hot flashes." on its home page. The first map suspiciously had arrows up and down, the crescent wrench-shaped road and a blue house with the cow-shaped mailbox.

When I clicked onto my destination, there were blinking graphics with a smiling hitchhiker pointing his thumb, a safety patrol pointing everywhere and a swimmer explaining a curve. A closer zoom revealed no traffic lights, my ex-husband spinning the map around and someone pointing to the ceiling.

Never mind anyone's directions, I thought. I just won't go. I'll probably get a flat tire anyway.

But I'll get even. The next time someone asks me for directions, there will be a yellow brick road, a cast of munchkins pointing everywhere and an evil stop light on the way to the Land of Oz.

# ALL iN a TWitter

I was among friends the other night when someone brought up the new tech term "twitter."

I took aspirin from my purse, held my jam-packed head in my hand and asked with faint brainwaves, "what on earth is that?" Not another high-tech something-or-other, I thought, and was weakened trying to comprehend.

Well, no one at the table knew, but all agreed that it was something. This, as I was just getting a grip about "blogs, bloggers and blogettes."

Blogs, of course, are the daily musings and additions to worldwide communications where at any given nanosecond, one can enhance and comprehend all information available out there. For instance, a daily blog might be an educated take on the economy, political tidbits or what Hollywood star just received a DUI. Or it might mean the current studies about men who snore too much.

Here a blog, there a blog, everywhere someone's blog. Once you read anyone's blog, then you are completely informed for that very nanosecond. But five minutes from then, it could all change.

Everyone knows that.

The blogger, furthermore, is that qualified person who writes about the stuff. He or she may not know what he or she is blogging about, but he or she certainly knows technology beyond the simple buttons that turn on computers. He or she knows the difference between Blackberries and blueberry pies. He or she certainly knows how to send texts that say, "where r u?" and respond, "buying T-paper, lol."

Everyone knows that.

The blogette might be a Radio City Music Hall dancer in a chorus line.

Or maybe a French bread lavishly slathered with butter and garlic to deliciously go with your New Year's resolution of a high-fat diet. Or, the blogette may be the slightly overweight person wearing pink.

So I certainly know all about blogs, feeling quite comfortable in my cyber knowledge. But the twitter? I guess that I'll have to look that one up.

So I got out my handy-dandy 20-pound Webster's Edition subtitled, Everything-But-What-You-Look-Up. It takes at least a half hour because I always get caught up on other interesting words like Timbuktu or titmouse. Then, of course, I am all atwitter because I've forgotten what to look up.

But, alas, the thing was published more than five minutes ago, so "twitter" still means something about a chirping bird.

"Chirps, cheeps, peeps and wings a-flap," are all related to the sounds that some people make when they can't seem to find their way in life.

Well, that makes sense. I feel that way every time I try to decide what to do when I grow up. The older I get, the fewer choices there are. I guess I should finally cut loose the ice skating Olympics goal or the one about being a ballet dancer. But there might be careers in the nursing home, after all.

I've also known lots of characters all atwitter about things. A friend's 94-year-old mother gets in a twitter when she must make major decisions like which way the mini-blinds should go. Or whether she should have tuna or chicken salad for lunch.

So now I think that my new career goal will be an official bloghag twitterer. It's not listed in the dictionary yet, so I will define it myself. The bloghag part must have at least three chins, wrinkles all over and falling body parts. Twittering must reflect absolutely no expertise, and be in constant confusion hour by hour. The computer entries will be bits and pieces of a hag clutching her throat all in a twitter.

# THe LocaL CHapter oF Crabgrasses

There's one in every neighborhood.

He stands at the property line guarding against any dangerous assaults to his yard. That would include a fleck of dandelion wafting his way or perhaps a flower-sniffing hag who prances about yakking cheerfully to other neighbors who might also send a fleck of dandelion wafting his way.

There's just too much light-heartedness, he might think, when invisible weeds are busy at work to wreak havoc on his perfect rectangular lawn. And the neighbors must all be guilty of being un-neighborly by seemingly not caring that he must routinely take a microscope to see if those windblown seeds with our identification nametags have taken root on his lawn.

The mean look on his face is directed at the rest of us disorderly gardeners that don't worry if blades of grass don't salute in perfect order. My neighbor calls him "Crabgrass." He performs dandelion-fleck duty at all times; the warm season is rough on a stiff like Crabgrass.

The winter season can be just as taxing for Crabgrasses of the world. If there's a flake of snow before dawn, he's out there with his bladed tractor to attack that major weather enemy that threatens his perfect cement. Once the drive is clear and dry, he gets into his perfect truck and glares at the rest of us who might throw a shovel or two around to make a few paths. One of our flakes may blow to his driveway, after all.

There must be other disapproving Crabgrasses on the block because as I exchanged plant cuttings with a neighbor the other day, curtains parted and ears cupped our way. I felt that I needed to provide the cupped ears with something scandalous. I wish my life were more interesting to them

63

than digging up "Lily of the Valley" to transplant, but I could provide no other juicy intrigues except that the magnolia tree was beautiful as the wind blew its petals their way.

The Crabgrasses probably belong to a local grassroots chapter of the Party of Crabs where they sit around with mean looks and discuss how undisciplined of neighbors to waste time being friendly to each other when there are dangerous rebels within the ranks of perfect grass.

The women Crabgrassettes tsk-tsk themselves into a state of cluck-clucking with hand-wringing helplessness about how the earth is much too dirty. They search for cleaner and more sanitary solutions to all that soil out there that might make its way into their houses. A neat polished rock is their environmental goal for the planet Earth.

"Compost pile" and "cow manure fertilizer" are banned phrases in this Party of the Crabs because the aforesaid substances are eyesores and nose sores to the neighborhood. They discuss how antisocial that some of us collect leaves and spread over the garden. A leaf might blow their way, it is warned. They all suffer that it is not possible to burn leaves, yard waste and various dandelion flecking neighbors at the stake.

The Crabgrasses also think that gardening tools of the trade like hoes, clippers and rose vases are frivolous and unnecessary to a garage collection. After all, any self-respecting Crabgrass needs only a carpenter's level for geometric bushes and a lawnmower with headlights to manicure the yard before sunrise. Then the rest of the day can be devoted to guarding against neighborly errant weeds.

Or maybe guarding against all those other rowdy activities like having a glass of wine on the front porch. Or laughing with another friend while not worrying about how the grass is perfectly uncut.

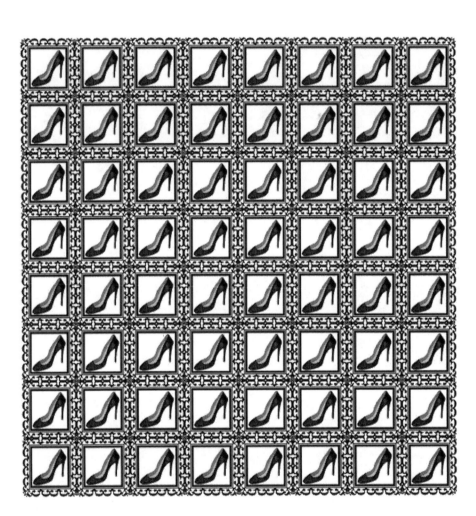

# THe LiFe aNd TiMeS oF WaLLpaper

Somehow the very word "wallpaper" always makes me laugh. Maybe because wallpaper has had such a legacy of mistakes in design judgment. Or maybe it can be overbearing in its presentation swallowing up a room in dark, gaudy effects. Or maybe "wallpaper" just looks funny in print.

There have been jokes about it – "I'm just a wallflower" and literary creations about going crazy into it – "The Yellow Wallpaper," by Charlotte Perkins Gilman in 1899.

I am more than sure, however, that wallpaper carries a bad name because of the 1950's. Those of us who remember that funky decade know that home design looked more like the Three Stooges were set loose in a rocket ship with plastic, Formica and vinyl.

And wallpaper. I was talking to a friend recently about our first day in kindergarten. It was a milestone event with its usual fears and tears. She and her fraternal twin were photographed in their living room before that first day.

"I've got to show you the photograph," she laughed, "you wouldn't believe the wallpaper!"

And we both laughed just thinking about our own wallpapered childhood. My grandmother used to wallpaper so often that eventually the structure of the house was held up by it. The design was always vertical rows with flowers and vegetation of sorts. Every year, the wallpaper paste man showed up to hang rows of garish blooms and branches of busyness. There were strawberries in the kitchen and ivy in the living room.

Actually, '50s aside, I was never much of a wallpaper fan. On my walls, I have always preferred art. And when I say "art," you must know

67

that my nose is in the air with careful consideration that "art" is elevated to snob status. So when I hang my children's fifth-grade framed watercolors of a ladybugs or a cheerful flower (isn't that art?), they are not eaten alive by rows of repeated hydrangeas or overbearing sunflowers.

But I got the yen a few years ago to wallpaper my bathroom. It would be harmless, I thought, and there would be no artwork to digest it. I spent so many hours with sample books that eventually my neck developed a tic. I finally chose dancing water lilies over a blue background.

Perfect for the bathroom. I would shower thinking that I was in a gentle waterfall in the tropics.

So, armed with directions and an enthusiastic "do it yourself" resolve, I headed upstairs. For some reason, I thought the bathroom ceiling should also have water lilies dancing about. My neck, still with the tic, turned into awkward nods as I tried to see the panels through bifocals.

The self-pasting strips became magnets as they traveled around the ladder, toilet and my stomach. OK, so the results weren't perfectly straight, but no one would see the pie slice behind the toilet or the fitted mosaic of leftover pieces under the light fixture.

Within a week, I realized that the background blue hue didn't match the floor tiles. Soon after, I thought that if I ever saw another water lily in my life, I might just wretch. I was in a bad mood of do-it-yourself failure every time I visited the bathroom.

I tore it all off except for a few stubborn pieces here and there. The bathroom looks much better now, unfinished and dull-walled.

If the '50s affair with wallpaper accomplished anything in my design life, it's that I hate wallpaper. I still see magazines with delicate rows of faint rose buds in bedrooms that make the walls seem so classy Victorian. I'm tempted sometimes, but remember the water lilies.

I'll stick to my grandchildren's artwork now.

# Declaring Waterbeds a Wash

I once had occasion to sleep on a waterbed. Or rather I should say "in" a waterbed, and I use the word sleep loosely.

It was unintentional, but necessary as the only motel room available at the time. The room was called the "honeymoon suite," according to the desk lady. What's that? I wondered. The only honeymoon I remember is the one to the sound of snoring or pages flipping.

The desk lady didn't snicker out loud but must have tittered at my flapping jowls, bifocals and rear end in the shape of the Super 8 sign in front. So I took the room because I had to.

Now that I look back, much of the reference to honeymoon simply means that it requires two people just to operate the machinery. I found that the Jacuzzi on/off button, for instance, was located across the room. This I noticed after I had gotten in to soak and steam, stood up to look for buttons and reread the directions. That required, of course, wandering about to find my glasses. The fine print, told me that the button was past the slippery tile to a dark corner. By then, my glasses had steamed up and I adjusted the timer button by Braille.

Had anyone seen my rear end teetering and touring the entire "suite," the honeymoon would have been immediately over. But I bubbled on…

Sure it was relaxing. For a few minutes. Then the lethargy stage set in, much like a cooked noodle. I was sinking fast into a helpless pile of jiggling and overheated organs with no muscle tone to ever stand up again. I don't remember the town I was in, but I imagined the local headlines saying something about "non-honeymooning hag drowns in her own sorrows."

So I approached the bed. Granted, my waterbed experience is limited because I always felt that there were already enough plumbing and heating contraptions in one household without adding another.

"Oh, Sue," they say. "It's just like floating." Yeah, right. If I actually floated, say on a cruise ship, it would require anti-nausea medication. Moreover, a bed that heavy would come right through the ceiling of an old house.

"Oh, no," say the snake oil salesmen, er I mean waterbed people. "The weight is evenly distributed blah blah blah." Weight is weight in my book, unless the rules of gravity have changed. If an evenly distributed elephant were placed on the second floor of my house, it would promptly collapse, trunk and all, into the living room below. Besides, I can personally lift a regular mattress, but not a waterbed.

But relaxed by the Jacuzzi and with book in hand, I approached the bed with an open mind. I sat on the edge and immediately lost my balance. It was either risk concussion on the tile side or dive into waves on the bed side. I dove, and by the time I found my bearings, I was bouncing belly up and staring at my own image. The nice overhead canapé was actually a mirror to send back a most horrifying reflection. (What is this mirror stuff, anyway?)

I avoided the mirror and tried to arrange my reading position. My rear end sank, stomach floated upward and dinner gurgled in limbo. There was no reading position to find. No sleeping position either because I just seemed to dog paddle about.

At one point, I needed to get up for something. With knees in my face, I hoisted myself not quite close enough to the edge to gain leverage and stand up. My right leg stretched too far and turned into a full-blown Charlie Horse. With my leg shaped like the boot of Italy, I limped around to regain control.

I'll take my own bed, thank you, that stands still and needs no heating elements, plumbing maintenance or extra medical services.

# Diva aNd tHe GLUe Factory

No, it's not the name of a new music group, not yet anyway. It's about a cat named Diva and where she might be next.

My repertoire of previous house pets, cats or dogs, have always been grateful for the creature comforts that I provided. The dogs thought that the back yard was high living with a juicy menu of sniffs at each grass blade. They always appreciated any color of food bag that came into the house. Hey! chicken pellets, that's great! Oh! beefy chunks! Wow!

And my dogs always thought it miraculous to be able to sit in the back seat with snouts pointed outward to cruise the foreign smells. The rattle of keys and shuffle of shoes meant great and grand things to them. They even learned to spell C-A-R.

My various cats thought the cat box to be luxurious living. Some ventured to the outside world to keep critters in check. Occasionally, something disgusting would drape from a cat's mouth to bring inside. I had to do frequent mouth frisks at the door. But the intent was honorable to protect the homestead against creepy things.

So then, all seemed to report to doggie heaven or cat demise about the same time. Since I've never lived life without four legs to greet me at the door or fur hairs on the couch, I opted to adopt.

The Humane Society failed to mention that Diva was an impossible wretch. I didn't notice it, but there was a skull-and-crossbones over her cage. She played the game, too, and buried her nose in my lap begging for a happy home, nice cat box and whatever food I presented. She promised to be good. I think I heard her say, "Yes, ma'am" with a halo over her fur. I took her and another one because two cats would keep each other company, joyous and friendly, sharing and caring.

71

They hated each other from day one. I've heard more meaty hisses from Diva's whiskers than I have heard from National Geographic documenting rattle snakes in Africa. She bristles in his presence and gets the creeps from her glaring face to her flipping tail. She even conspires to eat all the food so that he would starve.

OK, so they don't like each other. They can occupy different rooms and different couches. Then she went into her fussy diet phase when she wouldn't eat anything I put before her. The orange bag was no good, the green bag, the pink bag, the mature cat bag, all no good. If you put expensive olive oil over it, a little tuna juice, crack an egg, nothing. For a while I even cooked rice for added effect. It just made a mess on the floor. She was actually getting thin. Now I'm working on cans. Canned salmon, canned suspicious lumps, no lumps, different color.

Fresh tap water is also beneath her. She prefers the toilet or water from a plant tray.

Then she decided that the cat box was too low class for her. She preferred behind the water heater, washing machine or in some basement corner. Then the first floor was a better option. It would be handy and more convenient near her perpetual napping couch. She now visits the same corner in the living room, the same corner that I have scrubbed with ammonia after every "accident." Now I just leave the jar there.

Having her is like the "teachable moment" when we communicate with each other. She's learning to spell, G-L-U-E  F-A-C-T-O-R-Y! And I'm learning to hiss like the rattle snakes in Africa.

# ALL THat GLitters...

**i**s certainly gold. Bring on the glitters! It's that time of life.

I used to have a rather pragmatic approach about wearing a lot of jewelry. It had to do with my mother's natural beauty axiom, "beauty is as beauty does." And my stepdad's artless view of life that said women should be just plain and stand over the stove.

They obviously forgot the bit about chins that fall, skin that hangs and wrinkles that compete with mountainous ranges on any house globe.

But nevertheless, I went into the world in my 20s as if there were no tomorrow about natural soap-and-water beauty. I didn't look too closely in the mirror at the time because I had just recovered from a zit-infested teenage with some boils thrown in. But I dreamed on as I studied the fashion magazines that featured porcelain skin and flawless beauty.

So who needed that much jewelry?

Earrings, of course, were always an exception. They were hot commodities and choice purchases for any mood. They were standard therapy, listed these days in the shrink's reference guide for nontoxic medication to cure one's way out of any mental disorder. And the prescription is good most anywhere because everyone sells earrings – airports, drugstores or jewelry stores. And they don't have to be expensive gemstones, just any old hanging something-or-other will do.

At one time or another, I have managed to collect green elephants, dangling Christmas trees and mother-of-pearl pink lobsters from New England. There were the hippie-era feathers that reached the shoulder and gaudy gold round things about the size of a standard slinky.

Eventually, my earring collection grew to fit a room-sized hardware tool chest. I still roll it out occasionally to tour my many psychological

75

moods over the years. Everything from male disappointments to PMS conditions are in that collection.

About the time I was considering live fishbowl wires, I noticed that something was happening to the earring style. They were becoming smaller and more modest. A simple pearl or perhaps a small stud was in order.

That's fine for the natural beauty days and all those perfect models in the fashion magazines, but my wrinkles were appearing and everything was falling into crevices that looked similar to a weather map of mudslides. The mirror must be kidding!

So I gradually became interested in more glitter to deflect the damage. When I recently went to a wedding and stopped at my daughter's, I didn't realize just how glittery I had become. She put her sunglasses on and looked askance.

"Mom, is that you?" Then I gave her a complete tour of my jewelry from head to toe. There was a choker necklace with matching earrings, an Avon watch ring next to a pinky birthstone ring, a sparkly scarf draped over a beaded bodice and a gaudy broach. None of the colors matched, but there was glitter!

"I didn't think that you wore rings," she said. I explained that they covered my jagged nails from chewing and misshapen knuckles from years of nervously cracking.

"I've never seen you wear a necklace," she observed. I told her that I figured a dozen strands of something would cover about two chins. "And a sparkly broach?" she wondered. I explained that maybe the glare would divert attention from falling objects from there on down to the ankle bracelet designed to cover various corns and deformities. "The arm bracelet next to the cuff watch?" Well, they just looked good together.

I figure in another ten years I'll be glittering like the party disco ball, just to empty the trash.

# Forgetting About Alzheimer's

I t occurred to me the other day when I couldn't remember someone's name that I should do some serious thinking about the potential of developing Alzheimer's Disease.

I noticed that the disease has reared its forgetful head on both sides of my family. My uncle has not recognized his wife of 50 years nor grown children for some time. He has a delightful time in the home, however, and can't wait to board the bus for an outing at the zoo.

One of my grandmothers had a comfortable stay in a home where she completely forgot that two out of three of her sons died young. But the menu was wonderful, she reported, and so were the activities.

Then, another aunt socialized with the home's caretakers so much that she preferred their company to her five daughters whose names she couldn't remember, anyway.

Not to make light of a dark subject, but I thought the rule of memory is that when you change floors in your house, your brain stays on the first floor. Then you have to rewind your thought process to remember why you went upstairs to begin with. Was it to gather laundry, look for the cordless phone or find a toenail clipper?

Or when you open the refrigerator door and can't remember why? Come on, we have more important things to think about in life besides that jar of mayonnaise.

Or the proverbial car keys location? I'm sure that we who have misplaced them are safe and sane. Why, last week I misplaced my real estate tax bill. That's simply something that Mr. Freud would slip into the normal category, nothing disease-like.

My friends are also normal. They only choose to forget someone's name because it's fun to play "fill-in-the-blank" and Charades.

I just played the games with a friend yesterday. The opening dialogue began smoothly. She was about to tell me a story about someone that she had run into the other day whose name she couldn't remember.

"Oh, you know who I mean," she snapped her fingers. Give me a hint, I prodded.

"You know, whose husband you can't stand." The finger snapping continued and "you know" several times.

"It's coming now..." she was about to give birth. By then I was dancing around the room urging visual cues. "Is she fat? Was she wearing stripes?"

There was huge relief when we both remembered so-and-so's name. She forgot the story, however. But the conversation was fun, anyway.

This same friend, who only last year was a walking encyclopedic reference of gardening terms, referred to a flower as "you know, that pink thing." For the next hour, she became so obsessed about forgetting the name of the "pink thing," that she forgot where she had planted it.

We regular people can't possibly be expected to remember every minor detail that comes along. Like our children's names, for instance. We often have to go through a few prefix attempts before we get to the actual name. My children, for instance, are "Ja-Piper" and "Pi-Jason," just like my grandmother used to call me "Pat-Bet-I mean Sue Anna." Sometimes a dog's name would get in there.

Then I wonder about a few everyday basics, like did I or didn't I take my medication? Or, with the car running, why do I make three trips back to the house because I forgot something?

What really bothers me is the sight of my daughter's smirk, the kind that travels from her cheek to her ear. Then, "Mom, you already told me that story." OK, so it deserves another laugh.

So, I think I'm still safe from Alzheimer's. I remember my home address and have everything written on the calendar what I'm supposed to do next.

But, if I forget the location of my regular job...send me to the home. I'd rather go to the zoo, anyway.

# FoRM FoLLoWS FuNctioN

**U**se it or lose it, is the way it goes when it comes to our evolved selves. Everything from body parts to brain functioning is, fortunately or unfortunately, a reflection of what we do with them.

With that observation, it seems that humans have evolved to the present day with wisdom teeth that are no longer necessary for tearing up fast food or a tail bone with no function except to fall on now and then and have to stand around until it heals. For that matter, there are organs that we think we have outgrown, like those that cause appendicitis attacks or tonsils that seemed all the rage to remove at various times.

It will be interesting to see how the human body evolves in future archeological digs. That is, once the diggers get past the garbage bags designed to last thousands of years, or the outdated cell phones still attached to the skulls of users.

A layer beneath that will reveal only human remains shaped like office furniture that holds computers. Eye sockets will be enlarged to encase the permanent screen-popping boing-yoing eyeballs with no peripheral vision. The facial muscles will gradually disappear into staring mode, except an occasional scowl when the system is down.

From upper body to hand will be arms shaped like a computer mouse on the right and coffee cup on the left. No biceps will be necessary. Legs will rapidly become extinct from lack of use at the advent of chairs that roll from screen to refrigerator to microwave.

What archeologists and historians in the future digs might find interesting is that my ex-husband is single-handedly responsible for the first decline in human activity. Long before the computer age, Conrad Langencouch, declared exercise a form of media harassment. Having not the slightest inclination to move around, his deadpan comment was, "my body is just a cage for my head." This as he peered above an open book propped on his stomach.

He snickered at body builders and mused that their heads were proportionately too small for their greased muscles. He scoffed at joggers, runners and everything-elsers who had the nerve to look happy while exercising.

He detested bicycling and hiking. They seemed inefficient, especially when there's a perfectly good car in the garage for transportation. Lifting weights was dull and caused that unpleasant sweat.

He claimed that he got enough exercise crawling under the car to change the oil, carrying groceries to the house and reaching into his wallet. About the time that his hair disappeared, a protruding stomach appeared. His chest was sinking and his arms were shrinking. The stomach, he justified, was there for storage of beef and fat for the future. He might stand up some day, after all. It didn't seem to bother him a bit that his stomach arrived in the room five minutes before he did.

And so it was, Langencouch remained horizontal for much of the latter 20th century. By the time the computer age arrived, he quickly developed an aversion to them. There were no bolts to turn or oil to change. Besides, he couldn't hold the monitor properly to read on the couch.

Soon, Langencouch was rarely seen upright. The last time I saw him, there was nothing left of his body to determine any detail. He had turned into a horizontal book stand with a hairless dome overhead. His glasses prescription was thicker than the book that he held. If I remember correctly, he was reading about the healthy effects of exercise.

# Giving Thanks to the Turkey in Your Life

With bad news getting worse everywhere, most of us can still eke out something to be thankful for.

If there's still an un-foreclosed roof over your head that hasn't fallen in yet, then that's a good grace opener before a Thanksgiving feast. If you still have a job, then never mind the abusive boss or unpleasant co-workers, bend down at the workplace entrance today and kiss the ground before you enter. It might not be there tomorrow.

Then looking around the Thanksgiving table, be thankful that the turkey didn't flap its wings and flee from salivating dogs staring through the oven window or the official serrated knife zeroing in.

Most importantly, be thankful for the other turkeys in your life. There's got to be at least one at your Thanksgiving dinner. It might be a mother-in-law who insists that the dressing is not within the official approved family heirloom list. Or a father-in-law that comes harummphing through the door and remains toad-like in the chair snoring too loud.

It might be the pregnant daughter who found the last living doctor in the world to approve of pre-natal cigarettes. Or the son-in-law that suddenly wears a food critic hat and says there's too much vanilla in the sweet potato recipe. It might be the glaring rest of the table that disapproves of one lump found in your mashed potatoes.

Another turkey in your life might be a sister-in-law who gets a migraine headache at the mere sight of your table wine and insists that she must have a brain scan before dessert is served. She might be the one who attempts to garner family support to boycott your next holiday dinner. But then, she might be severely ill by then.

Which brings to mind a favorite turkey that a classmate and I have to reminisce and snicker about. The ultimate hypochondriac in question lives on medical disability with a rare disease and resides in a wheelchair as we speak. She probably puts on theatrical makeup to feign hopelessness as she collects her check from the mailman.

My favorite turkey that we must discuss every year is the cousin who showed up drunk and wearing pink spandex at her father's morning funeral service. It's a holiday ritual not to let that one go by the wayside!

Another turkey in your life might be a son's girlfriend who is severely allergic to a single dust mite and cannot make it through the front hallway. Then once recovered from a sneeze attack, she stiffens into an icy glare at a possible future mother-in-law who refuses to put the wine glass down long enough to hang her jacket.

And the turkeys go on. As quickly you meet and befriend people or marry others, the more turkeys there are to acquire.

My ongoing personal turkey happens to be an ex-husband that never seems to be absent from a holiday gathering. While many don't speak to exes, I still notice mine when he roars through the back door like a balding boomerang whose beard gets whiter each year. He hum-drums into the room with the same commanding nervous habits he always had. Soon the cupboards open and slam with rhythmic annoyance as he complains about ex-wives who don't organize properly. "Where's this?" and "Where's that?" while he worries that there is probably dust under the refrigerator.

But I'm still thankful to have this turkey in my life. It is truly a blessing to have someone to laugh about and freedom of the press to pass it along.

# AN Elevating Idea For MS. Otis

I stepped into an elevator the other day and found myself pushing buttons for everyone's floor. I was immediately emboldened to imagine myself as the new Ms. Otis with the important job of taking others to their locations.

Then I forgot that the second floor is as high as my fear of heights will take me. I once looked out my attic window and suddenly felt queasy. I have been known to crawl on all fours down the aisle of the balcony of the theatre.

So when I turned around in that elevator, someone asked me if I remembered the old manual operators donned with the caps and uniforms that portrayed official grandeur. He probably glanced at my stack of chins and saw that I would probably remember that and perhaps the days of horse and buggy, as well.

My elevator days are long over, however, especially after horrifying terrorist ideas that go after tall buildings. In my youth, things were different. Yes, I was atop the Empire State Building in the pre-World Trade Center days when a mere ledge prevented people from leaping to their deaths. At 18, I might have used that as a solution to solve my zits problems.

On that same high school senior trip, I had whipper-snapper blood pressure and heart rate to swiftly climb the Washington monument without flinching. I also waved from the Statue of Liberty with fearless abandon. If it were inordinately windy up all those stories, we just giggled ourselves into oblivion and imagined how it would be to fly across Manhattan using pleated skirts for sails and teased hair for altitude.

By the time I took an elevator up to the top of The John Hancock building in Chicago, I had graduated into keeping my feet as near ground as possible. It's a new disorder called "Otis-cide's Syndrome by Proxy," or the temptation to jump because of a hangnail. Or just to test some designer label wings without considering the consequences.

I am also troubled with the idea that all tall buildings are engineered to swing back and forth, a reality that can manifest itself with whitecaps in the toilet water. Ok. Slight exaggeration. I know all about the explanation, but I just don't swing with buildings.

So in my fearless days, I guess I missed my youthful chance to apply for the job of Ms. Otis. It must have been a fine job then because that operator stayed in the building for years and knew everyone on a first name basis, as well as the floor to go to. I also remember the job as having to apply a bit of skill to get exactly level to the floor. Had I done that, I'm sure that I would have jutted the passengers to death trying to align that exact inch.

Or, "Tenth floor; mountain climb, ninth floor; jump for your life!" Then there are all those horror stories about elevator cables that broke, or simply got stuck somewhere while the building was swinging back and forth.

The good part is that you get fun information from people. I had an elevator man once poll everyone going up and down to advise him how to greet the First Lady.

Though the job is long gone in favor of magic buttons, it should still be available for those with "Otis-cide's Syndrome by Proxy." I could yak and be a hero button pusher. And if someone asks for higher than the second floor, I can say, "Are you nuts? The building swings back and forth up there!"

# Having a Handy Home Solici-Zapper

I t's the newest form of phone technology that I am holding out for.

The way it works is that when a phone solicitor dials your home number, the barrel of a gun comes out the other end and blows the caller into oblivion. Or, for those with a bit less violent nature, a gadget might be that at the first sound of "Congratulations, you have won…" a fly swatter thwaps the face of the caller, or pepper spray.

Right up there with murder and terrorism is phone solicitation. I'm sure that the dialers wear black hats, molest children and are probably rude at funerals. They are likely as sensitive as a wooden block and look creepy. In fact, are they really people, or a technological voice byte?

Maybe somewhere there is an Annoying University where people learn to bother others by intruding upon their lives on a daily basis. They must practice the most obnoxious tone of voice, the least interesting speech and act mournful when refused.

Or perhaps there are newborns with rubbing palms waiting to jump from the nursery to annoy the next newborn and try to sell the latest rage in formula. Then they grew up ugly with mothers who dressed them funny.

Maybe, somewhere out there in cyber-space is a Wicked Witch of Central Standard Time that stirs a cauldron steaming of fresh boiled telephone numbers spiced with incorrect surnames.

The very dictionary word "solicit," in fact, uses descriptions like coercion and pressure, with some lesser definitions that pertain to more low life activities. Thank you, I don't need coercion or pressure to buy or do anything when I am in my own house. The whole point to having a place to live is to have a sanctuary AWAY from all those aggravating pressures of real life.

But, sure enough, at any hour seven days a week are cheerful greetings that begin with, "Hello Mrs. Larggerbergerdorfski, how are you today?" Or the predictable three seconds before a recording kicks in.

Next on the offensive list of intruders are the canvassing door-knockers who have something to sell or promote. For them, I want an enormous skull-and-crossbones sign at the mailbox that says "Death to those who ring or knock." While I'm in the shower, I'm not interested in anything out there that the world has to offer. Once, I came home from a very long workday and as I got my mail, two smiling men in pleasant suits carrying brochures headed for the porch.

"NO THANK YOU!" my megaphone voice echoed up and down the block. They meekly tip-toed to the next porch and hoped that my neighbor was friendlier. (I told the story to my "do unto others" mother – she was mortified that a daughter of hers could be so unmannerly.)

The ultimate offense happened one sunny morning when I took an exercise walk in the park. A solicitor caught up with me to try to convince me that I should attend some church or another. I felt a most un-Christian mood rising that a stranger would accost me about what I do in life. It ruined an otherwise nice day to enjoy the fresh air.

Then, there are the forests of junk paper that travel from mail box directly to the trash can in the same minute. While there is at least no human to deal with, the junk mail stills accumulates. I once lost an entire frozen pizza on the counter underneath a recent trip from the porch.

Solicitor, beware of Mrs. Larggerbergerdorfski!

# Here's Mud in Your Eye

I t's a toast to all those unfortunate souls who had to put their lives on hold and try to beat back the determined waters of Mother Nature. Sometimes, Noah's Ark sails right past us when we have nothing to spare. If you are high and dry, relish every moment until next time. If not, toast to better times.

I was lucky this time and toasted a couple friends recently. We agreed that sometimes it's just pure lottery that keeps the river from the door. But not so fast...

I took laundry to the basement a few days ago and was first assaulted by the smell of a sunken ship, circa Grover Cleveland era. My basement is normally not exactly a finished level fit for the Home and Garden Television Channel. It's just a plain basement with a cement floor, rough walls, ungainly furnace, octopus pipes reaching in every direction and enough spider webs to populate an entire reference of arachnophobia.

But where did the Good Ship Lollipop sink? It seemed suspiciously in the cat box area. Cat boxes, of course, are standard equipment when you have various personalities roaming about the house. My house contains a "Diva" who drapes herself in predictably serene places. On the couch, under the couch or exactly on the crossword puzzle in front of you. "Tripod," on the other hand, was a shelter kitten recovering from a car hit and left with three legs. He is by no means handicapped, however, because he flies through the room, hunts mice and ingests unfortunate insects with lightening speed.

Both of them require a cat box that resembles the latest "Better Homes and Gardens" bathroom upgrade. If there's a minor flaw, then their claws turn to garden shovels and carefully scoop the litter to the floor around it.

With pursed lips and dainty paws, they are determined to use a box that is exactly to their standard.

What all this box stuff has to do with floods is that with half the bag of litter on the outside, water came from the wall. That is, the same wall that I have repaired and cleaned the eaves, had a tile dug and conducted an exorcism to rid the Wicked Witch of the West from raining in my basement wall.

The end result of seeping water and litter looks like something out of a '50s science fiction where some garish green bubbling slime kept spreading with viral speed to attack innocent victims like hags with too much to do besides shovel the basement.

All is not lost, however, since it's rather admirable to learn from each experience. Scoopable cat litter, for those who are not well-versed in the adventures of the cat box, is engineered to suck up everything from liquid to nearby objects. Each kernel is like a thirsty Quaker Oat after sitting in milk too long. The end result is a polite and evenly textured mud.

So rather than having to mop water, you just shovel mud neatly onto newspaper, preferably the section that would carry such a ridiculous column as this. For this cleanup technique, refer to the familiar dog accident method with two pieces of card board and a strong stomach. If you've never cleaned up the cat box or a dog accident, then you have built no character in life.

Once the cleanup is accomplished, then you are merely left with a discolored floor, shoes that must be trashed and the sunken ship odor that will remain until the next draught scheduled for whenever the calendar calls for the next disaster.

But meantime, toast yourselves for surviving another day on this perilous planet.

# Home Again, Home Again, Jiggity Jig

It is possible that your own driveway is the main road hazard when it comes to car travel. This after surviving regular highway perils out there that would include canyon-sized potholes, smirking state troopers with radar and serial killers looking for hags with several chins.

Not to mention those other impolite drivers that think they own the road. Or deer that choose your exact global position at that very moment to mosey across the road, pose with pursed lips and stare into your headlights.

Or gas prices, but that's another story.

I drove home in the wee hours the other night after a one-day serving of Mother Nature's wild fluctuations of weather. There was every form of precipitation from rain to sleet to flakes. The roads had been probably taken care of; piece of cake. My driveway, however, was poised for hazard.

There was a sheet of ice thick enough for your average hockey game. In fact, had I not been already delusional from driving late at night, I would have sworn that Olympic skaters were practicing axels until my headlights scared them off.

All would be fine if the driveway were simply flat and, snow or ice, you could just tip toe your tires to the garage like a normal person. Mine, however, is a steady incline to the garage at some degree of angle that I was supposed to learn back in high school geometry. That teacher some 40 years ago drew one on the chalkboard and warned, "Never have a driveway with this steep incline." She glanced at me, but I thought nothing of it because geometry didn't interest me, so I didn't listen.

The rest of the class did and I'm willing to bet that they went on to lead normal lives with flat driveways these days. And I further assume that those same classmates pull into their driveway saying, "ah, home again, home again, jiggity jig," get out of the car and calmly walk into the house. Moreover, I think that those same classmates dream at night about that zit-infested dizzy tall girl shaped like Olive Oyl with big feet from their geometry class and how she has probably destroyed the front end of her car from the ungainly speed bump at the bottom of the driveway.

The fact is, part by part, the front end of my car has gradually disappeared from taking a running start to defy the snow and ice. Then I once ran into someone's parked car sliding down where my tires were still and the car kept moving. That's the way I tell the story, anyway, but my daughter reminds me that I wasn't looking but rather glaring at the house that was glaring back at me. But her version of my hitting the car has no credibility since she side-swiped the garage every time she pulled out. At least I was a good Samaritan and left a note on the damaged car.

So with imaginary whirling axels on the icy driveway, I tried not to wake the neighborhood with spinning wheels and swearing phrases. But worse, with the car on the street, I had to make it up the ice rink on foot. There were two choices available; take a side route on the neighbor's icy yard or do acrobatic maneuvers over my railroad tie landscaping.

That same night, my geometry teacher and snickering classmates probably dreamed that a menopausal Olive Oyl was arrested for suspicious behavior singing, "Home again, home again, jiggity jig."

# Bah Halloweenbug!

try not to be an old sourpuss in life, but sometimes I can't help myself when it comes to Halloween.

Actually, I've never been a fan of Halloween. I ran a mostly sugarless, junk foodless and pop-less household for my children. While that may seem like a tough regime, I don't think that it's child abuse to have only milk, juice or water available. My theory was that if cookies and candy weren't in the house, then there was nothing to argue about. My husband, however, occasionally stashed a few Hershey's kisses in his toolbox.

So here comes Halloween and, for the price of one baboon costume and many a "treat or treat," there would be enough cache of sweets to turn any ordinary functioning child into a sugar-crazed trampoline junkie for a week. Anyone who has ever taught anything from kindergarten to ballet class knows how dysfunctional a sugared up child the day after Halloween.

And somehow, "trick or treat" sounds suspiciously like an assault -- "trick" (threaten harm) or "treat" (your wallet). But then the mean trick-or-treatees came back with more crimes, like razor blades in apples or some such unthinkable act. And the whole thing escalated into a potential terrorist act.

Though I admit a few tears when my firstborn wore his little bear outfit to a porch light next door, I worry now that we teach our children the basics of greed. Some older children don't even bother to wear a costume. They just roam the neighborhood looking for whatever freebies are out there. There's not even a "Thank you" or "(hee hee) trick or treat." Just run to the next porch carrying a room-sized bag.

95

If we had stuck with the innocent spirits and magic of All Hallow's Eve, or All Saint's Eve, the October event sandwiched without fanfare between full moons and falling leaves might still be fun. Like don a sheet with slits cut out for the eyes or tiptoe about in a ballet tutu with pink slippers. I remember a costume contest in junior high school. My mother was most inept about needle arts, so there was no sewing machine in the house to stitch up a creative costume. I wore a store bought cat-like outfit with stripes and a tail, but since it was cold, I had to open my jacket and top it off with a goofy grin that said, "Guess what I am."

What I remember most about that contest, however, was a class mate whose costume was constructed out of shoeboxes and hardware paraphernalia that looked like an awkward astronaut stomping across the moon. He won, and I was jealous that his mother was so creative.

And our "tricks" were little more than soaping a window or two. I think that was before the contemporary "TP-ing" house prank where one modest roll of toilet paper turns into a forest of hanging tissue. I remember once that the morning after Halloween, a wayward outhouse found itself under the traffic light in the main intersection of town.

The worst thing about Halloween is how it has escalated into a major industry. As soon as the summer grills disappear, the lantern lights, witch paraphernalia and spider webs appear. And aisles of terrorist-free candy, of course. No lawn should be without a cemetery stone or two with RIP on it. That's to make sure that we continue spending money between summer and Christmas.

So Halloween is one night in the year when my porch light stays off and I hide in the dark from phony festivities. May this holiday RIP!

# Horse Thieves of a New Age

In the old days of the Wild West, the horse thief was the lowliest character around. He was a "no good, dirty rotten scoundrel," according to cowboy lore.

A thief in any century is pretty low, especially when you consider the "premeditating" part. That means that someone actually rubs palms, shifts eyes back and forth and thinks mean thoughts beforehand.

The murderer, on the other hand, while still committing a most distasteful act, might be innocent one minute and passionately committing the act of murder the next. As a crime of passion, it may require no previous mean thoughts. If someone wearing a black hat, for instance, leaped from the bushes and shouted, "Ha, ha, you're ugly and your mother dresses you funny," I might entertain a brief murderous thought. Especially if he stuck his tongue out and with a Bronx cheer said, "and you're a total failure." But most of us have a conscience that keeps us from crossing that line from hostility to murder.

Most of us have been tested at various times in life, especially those of us who have been through a goofy husband who mows down flowers or nervously cleans and throws out a valuable magazine.

But back to Wild West horse thieves. Butch Cassidy and his like were actually making rather intelligent choices about steeling horses. After all, the horse was a reliable source of transportation. Unlike the car, its lifespan was 25 to 30 years. In the meantime, it merely needed water and an open pasture for refueling. It was bought and sold on a handshake with no registration papers or license plate required for its rear end. Its hooves were rated not to go flat for a lifetime and needed no muffler for its rather pleasant clip clop through town. It always started in hot or cold weather and needed very little parking space.

A few clicks from the side of the mouth and a little TLC and, hey, horse thieves had themselves some quality transportation. The journey may have been slow and dusty, but the horse thieves galloped to the end of the day, threw the reins over the tavern post and moseyed in for a beer.

The carjacker of today, however, must have an IQ of about room temperature to think that stealing a car is a valuable prize. Depending on how much gas is in the tank, the joyride may end in the next block. If there's gas until the next state, then the reality sets in only later.

"Hey, Man, have you got gas money?"

"No, you Idiot, what's the engine light blinking for?"

After that, Man and Idiot may as well rob the nearest bank for gas, steal some more for parts, murder the insurance agent and hold up the mechanic at gun point. That's a full time job before the seat belts are even clicked.

If the stolen prize is a new car, it will lose value by the time the thieves drive through for fast food. If the season is summer, the air conditioning will need work. If the season is winter, everything will need work. The oil may need changing, the battery gets old and the tires need replacing. The rust is rusting, and the exhaust is exhausting.

Even the joyride is without joy. There are speed limits, speed traps, traffic bottlenecks, bad roads and bad drivers.

"Hey Man, there's a cop on our tail."

"Shut up, you Idiot, I'm trying to find a way to move this seat back. Next time, we'll steal from someone with longer legs."

# In Praise of Procrastination

One glorious reason to grow up and graduate to an empty nest is that we no longer have to repeat ourselves ad nauseum about life's little lessons – monitoring the chores, reminding about laundry and nagging about homework.

"Later, mom" I heard all too often about homework and "sometime" from my son. "Later" really meant "probably never" and "sometime" meant "when the mood strikes."

An even better reason to graduate into an empty nest is that no one monitors MY behavior. I used to hear all that virtuous prose punctuated with musical notes and delivered in rhythm. "Never put off until tomorrow that which you should blah blah blah," said my grandmother. And "A stitch in time saves nine," said some aunt.

Another favorite delivered with a wagging finger is, "The early bird gets the worm." That is if, I muse, a morning person bird happens upon a lazy oversleeping worm. Or perhaps a Type A personality bird stalks an underachieving worm.

"Early to bed, early to rise makes a man healthy, wealthy and wise." That healthy, wealthy and wise man, by the way, surely must have a wife on staff to cook and clean for him while he beds and rises early.

I've decided that life isn't quite as simple as all that rhyme and prose. Those above generations were so busy living up to some ethereal set of values for tomorrow that they forgot how to live today. The bed had to be made almost before you woke up. An unmade bed for five minutes bordered on heretical behavior. So what if the bed remains unmade for half a day or even, shockingly, a whole day? Do you go to housekeeping jail? Does lightening strike? After all, I don't give tours of my bedroom.

When I hosted holiday dinners, my mother-in-law (somewhere up there in dishwashing heaven) would practically remove the dirty dishes from the table before I announced that "the dishes aren't going anywhere, but the conversation is." Or before the gravy was passed around. I know that she thought I was a fallen woman, but I was used to pleasantries and thought it more important to enjoy guests than to jump up and do housework.

I have made a new decision these days that I don't procrastinate, I prioritize. Prioritization is the real reason that my bed is currently unmade. And the laundry sits in the dryer wrinkling. There might be a cat hair or two in the den. I'd rather write this column than nervously prepare for a "Better Homes and Gardens" tour.

Multi-tasking is part of prioritization. If there are several things that need to be done, I sit down and read a book. That takes care of mental health. If we rush around and prepare for tomorrow, we don't live today. My mother always had this "get it over with" idea. The trouble with that is that dishes, laundry and housekeeping are never "over with." I think her funeral will be "over with" before she arrives.

So I say at lot of "later" these days. No one arrests me or recites poems. The bed doesn't run away, the clothes might have a few wrinkles, the leaves will be there next spring ready to rake, the spaghetti sauce gets better later and wine improves with time. What's wrong with a little "later?"

Just don't tell my children.

# In Search of the Designer Parking Place

A friend of mine happens to be the only living person in North America to have bought a new car recently. Right off the lot, it comes complete with the expensive car scent, Global Positioning System and automatic latte brewer with or without a sprig of vanilla.

She thought about ordering a locater system, but didn't want anyone to locate her at the shoe store.

Naturally, she is rather particular about where she puts her new prize, all shiny and bright, in a parking lot. It's an experience that I have never had. "Let's just put it here and hope we don't get a ticket for having too much rust in a public place," I always offer.

So we circled the mall the other day for a half hour in her new car until she settled on a spot. It wasn't near traffic, it wasn't too close to the next car and she could have the yellow lines exactly parallel to the sales rack. I had to dangle myself upside down underneath the passenger side, in fact, with an engineering instrument to report the location of the yellow lines.

I took aspirin from my purse on the way into the store to get the blood back from my head. She walked backwards looking longingly toward her precious car parked on the end. I think I heard it say that it would be fine at the lock click. Then, she gently blew a kiss.

When she parks her new car on the street in front of my house, she must do background checks for everyone on my block. She also makes sure that our odd/even days are correct. With her GPS, she can crosscheck the exact date with the side of the street. Feeling sure that her car is safe from birds overhead, she heads for my door.

It was my first experience in life about designer parking spaces. Having lived in a big city for a spell, I learned that any parking place that pops up is a good thing. With money already in the meter, it's jackpot. You also learn to warp your way into a shoebox using the gentle touch tone method. Thud! "Oh whoops." Thud! "OK, we're in."

I was parallel parking, in fact, with this friend when she announced that she could never do that. I breezed over it, pretending great expertise, when suddenly slammed us upon the curb nearly setting off the airbags. Two women at a picnic table clutched their throats and glared.

I have also learned a level of parking place rage that comes naturally when in the city. On a recent trip, I found myself shouting at drivers for just being there. Once when I returned to my parking place, an arrogant driver simply doubled parked blocking me, left his car running and calmly moseyed into a store. I told him that I intended to call a tow truck. He shrugged and said, "go ahead" with every ounce of superiority he could muster. With that, I became enraged and ordered the tow. But, alas, by the time it showed up, the arrogant, superior, double parking moseyer had driven away, leaving my blood pressure elevated.

Actually in the city, parking spaces are more like prime real estate. After a major snow storm, we would all carve out our personal spaces with much labor. So no one came along to steal our shoveled effort, we would put various chairs and furniture as a sign of, "dibs." A city friend of mine photographed his couch on the snowy street as part of a family album, fondly recalling the designer parking place.

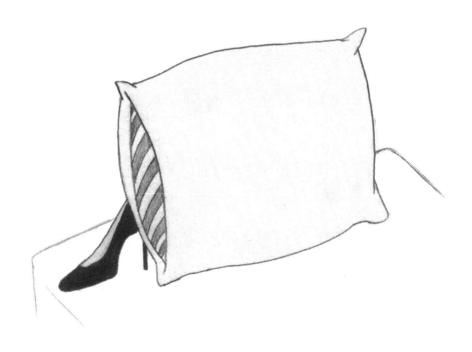

# Banking on the Tooth Fairy

Income from the tooth fairy was my first financial windfall. It was a whole quarter, shiny and solid found beneath my pillow one Sunday morning in the second grade. That year, with my extra quarter in my piggy bank, my school picture looked like a jagged-toothed wolf in pigtails.

Then with inflationary tooth fairies of the time, my next windfall was in the third grade with a fifty cent piece. That was big money then, with its etched eagle and solid silver promise. A half dollar weighed heavily in your pocket and went far at the dime store.

That was my last real income that meant meaningful profit. Unless you count, of course, the 50-cents-per-hour babysitting income here and there in high school. But expenses kept up at the same time because there was always a new shade of white lipstick to buy.

I got my first job, and it's been down hill ever since.

These days, financial profit still requires the banking services of the tooth fairy. She flies past, invisible, with imaginary money whipping around in the imaginary e-atmosphere creating assets in your mind only. And there are no coins under the pillow to prove that you actually have physical money.

I think I heard a tooth fairy flit past the other day. I was going to tell her that I was out of the losing teeth business but would be happy to have her services later when they fall out. She waved her wand and said, "Sell."

So I propped my feet up on the desk and phoned my broker. He also had his shiny shoes on the desk and leaned back with his designer three-piece suit and conservative tie. His costume and glass desk meant that I would be instantly rich along with all his other clients that believe pigs fly.

I had a slick look on my face and talked from the side of my mouth.

I, too, was dressed to get rich. I had on my thread-bare sweat pants with holes in the back, seedy tee-shirt that read the name of the last dead end job I had and worn sneakers, green with grass stain.

"Sell," I said with a sophisticated tone that meant great things in my bank investments.

"Sell what?" he was aghast. Oh, whoops. How do you define "assets" again? He carefully explained that in order to sell something, you have to have something.

I forgot about that. I went through the list of my assets and was prepared to have the upper hand. What does a goofy broker know, anyway?

"I'll have you know," my head swiveled, "I have more leftover knitting yarn in six different baby colors than the nearest yarn shop." I looked around for more assets. "Furthermore," I continued, "the contents of every room in this house is worth all the king's men on E-bay with a clawed tub thrown in."

I was on a roll now. "If I sold all my out-of-print books about 19th century operas and Mrs. O'Leary's cow in Chicago, someone in this country would pay premium for these finds. Even my tooth flossers are high-end quality. Sell!"

I guess my broker hung up. The tooth fairy flew away.

One of these days, maybe I'll actually have some of those flush funds, toilet securities or striped tube stocks to brag about. Then I can sell my irresponsible debt and have more money than I can find. Meantime, I am waiting for the tooth fairy to flit back into my life when my teeth fall out.

# INFLueNZa aNd tHe NaKed Lady

The following is – honest 'injun – a true story:

There are a lot of legitimate reasons for calling in to miss a day at work. The insurance companies know for sure, in fact, from their studies and statistics that prove lost work time related to health issues. There are the cigarette studies, of course, that drain medical insurance with health-related issues. There might be a work-related injury, or home accident. Giving birth is always understandable.

In my own studies, called Radar for the Ridiculous, there are some other common reasons to call in for a day off. There's the early call that says in a weakened voice, "I have the flu." There is also the occasional hysterical cell phone call that says, "I hit a deer and totaled the car." Bad luck, have the day off. I once left a message on the work phone that said, "I'm tired, have PMS and hate everything, so I won't be in." I think that they were glad.

Then there are always a few party revelers along the way to spice up the work gossip. One staggered in the door and goosed a co-worker. He was quickly escorted out after her scream was heard two departments away. Another giddy worker fresh from the bar flirted his way in, then couldn't wield a pen to sign in. He was requested to go home "sick."

Then there is the one about the naked lady in the field. That's right. The naked lady in the field. I'm sure that we've all used that excuse at one time or another.

It happened not long ago when a co-worker was up early getting ready for work. He accidentally locked himself out of the back door. While fiddling with the key, he thought that he saw a deer flitting in the corner of his eye. No, he was wrong. A second look revealed that it was a naked lady in the field.  She approached him as he nervously tried to unlock the door.  With his back to her – and that's the real answer to the cynical question about why he didn't see the color of her eyes – he thought surely that the naked lady was in some sort of peril.  He was about to offer a blanket, but when he turned around, she had vanished.

By then, he was shouting to his wife upstairs that he was locked out.  "You're not going to believe what just happened, but..." he called.  It's a story that no one is quite ready for first thing in the morning.  A call to police, however, verified that there had already been another call about this particular naked lady – not to be confused with the naked ladies that the rest of us have called in about.  Why, in fact, last summer, there was a naked man in my tomatoes.  He seemed polite enough but couldn't explain why he was there gazing at the zucchinis.

And so, why, did this co-worker miss the whole day at work instead of the few minutes on the phone with the police?

"Oh, you see, I had to remove the doorknob and couldn't leave the house open all day."

I think the real story is that his wife wouldn't let him out of the house.

# Just Desserts For the Finicky Eater

I was having a pleasant Sunday breakfast recently with my daughter and new son-in-law at a local restaurant. We had just returned from the buffet table with our plates full of all the pretty colors of breakfast choices. What a delightful morning, I thought, to enjoy an outing with fresh brewed coffee and good food.

Then she became stricken. The air stood still at our booth as her face froze. Her brow was set, nose wrinkled upward and lip curled as she clutched her chest. Her eyeballs were enlarged. I kept on eating.

My son-in-law paled and became instantly concerned as if there were a choking emergency. I could tell that he was new at this. After 23 years of doing hard time with a finicky eater, I knew that this was no emergency. It was just another routine meal when she thought that she had been served arsenic.

I actually think that she was born that way. Though I never reported it to the LaLeche League at the time, I am probably the only mother of a newborn in captivity whose breast milk was the wrong flavor.

Since she couldn't articulate the word "no," for about two years, she had to resort to other food-refusal techniques. She developed teeth as early as possible. They were shaped like a saber-toothed tiger. Luckily, I managed to escape serious injury as I weaned her.

Then she hated her first solid foods. From cupboard to refrigerator, I would carry her around for a complete tour of the kitchen. I sang cheerful melodies about crackers and played airplane-hangar with applesauce. Her little dimpled arm turned into a fly swatter.

"Shall we have this?" I offered cooked carrots.

SWAT!

109

"Shall we have that?" I went for the peanut butter.

SWAT!

"Or, how about cheese?"

SWAT!

At nine months, I felt that she was ready for her own apartment. But I was brave and kept her around for another 18 years.

At restaurants, she would charm the waitress with normal behavior and big blue eyes. At four years old she would point to the most expensive thing on the menu. Then when her plate came, she would stare at it in horror. I remember whispering threats through clenched teeth across the table that I was going to "SHOVE those green beans down your throat if you don't pick up that fork NOW!"

Then there was the cereal stage. She thought that the seven food groups meant seven kinds of cereal. And whatever flavor of expensive boxed air with cartoons on the cover currently in the house was exactly the kind that she didn't want. That same arsenic-stricken look would overcome her as the groceries came in the house.

"Mom," she was weak with impatience. "I don't like that kind." But you ate snap, crackle and pop last week, I reminded her. No, she had a sudden distaste for snap, crackle and pop this week.

Then she would stare blankly into a bulging refrigerator that could hardly be closed because there was so much food. If I rattled off several menus that I planned to cook that week, she became hostile.

She seemed to thrive and grow, however, with a cereal bowl attached to her lower lip. She hardly noticed Thanksgiving dinner on the dining room table while she filled her cereal bowl.

The tough-loving parents, of course, always have the firm answer for the finicky eater. The proud advice begins with, "Why, in MY house..." then continues to an air-tight discipline about how their children must eat whatever is put before them. To my older one, this approach worked. I would broadly announce that such-and-such was, "on the menu for supper, the next meal is breakfast." He chose to eat rather than starve until the next day.

She preferred starving. By the time she was in high school, I had given up on including her on the grocery list. She subsisted on hair-care products alone.

By the end of our Sunday morning breakfast, I was helpless with laughter. The waitress finally asked me what was so funny.

"I don't have to take her home!"

# Just Your Average GOSSIP

One good thing about summertime is talking to your neighbor over the fence. We reconnect after a long winter, chit-chat about life and exchange fresh-picked vegetables.

And GOSSIP!

The very word conjures up images of immoral activity that I was warned against when I was young. Ah, "buzz buzz buzz," I tease, and I can just hear some graves spinning two states away because of such illicit behavior.

"Mind your own business," they always said.

"No, I'm not interested in anyone's affairs," my aunt would stiffen with her nose in the air. In the next breath, she would lower her voice and comment about how, "so-and-so looks like she's gained weight and perhaps pregnant buzz buzz buzz..." And her eyes shifted and ear cupped.

There's that old altruistic proverb that great people talk about ideas, others talk about things and lesser people talk about people. A friend said that if she wanted to hear gossip about family, she would call one sister. But she'd call her other sister when she wanted to talk about interesting ideas.

Another overweight friend complained that her also overweight sister was always telling the rest of the family how overweight she was. And on and on in the workplace about everyone else who can't do this or that.

How low class, my parents would think. I guess, according to them, we're supposed to wander around in a nun's habit mumbling Plato.

Let's face it. We all talk about everything! And, as human beings, we love every minute.

In the media, gossip is properly called "investigative reporting," or "television magazines." That's where we peer into other private lives and learn about their dysfunctions and closet skeletons from family murderers to one who murders families. And we call that, "education," as we rub our palms in fascination of the next person's woes.

Or the talk-show guest whose horrific story is told to, "prevent this from happening to someone else." Then mention nothing about the impending book and millions to be made because we can't wait to savor every detail of the sleaze.

I remember where I was for the entire nation's gossip from O.J's trial decision to CNN's last interview with Tammy Faye Whoever-she-married.

Down the social ladder after investigative reports to educate us, there's a term called, "schmoozing." That's when we carry on breezy and innocent conversation at the end of a workweek. It is pleasant dialogue and supposed to be stress-free beginning with tomorrow's diet and reading an interesting book.

But inevitably schmoozing turns to gossip in one sentence as innocent as, "I ran in to so-and-so the other day." Who was she with? What was she wearing? Was she fat? And the room leans forward for the real juice.

Actually, we all have embraced gossip quite naturally. It is the stuff of Shakespeare and likely before him. The classics immortalize adulterous and murderous behavior because we humans seem to enjoy it as a form of entertainment. We laugh, cry and feel passion in theatre, social functions and in front of the television.

So what I'm really doing is educating myself by reading Shakespeare, and watching an investigative report so that I can better communicate with people about how we can prevent scandalous behavior within ourselves. Sometimes I have to use examples about people I really know. It's not really gossip.

# Two-timing the Clock

When it comes to ticking clocks, I have one in every room. I relish the Roman numerals, woody faces and wrist creations – every one of them a fun creature comfort. Some have a soothing rhythm of ticking and others just serenely move along.

Telling time is no problem, either. For many, however, reading a clock is another story. It seems that once we all make it through the first grade and discover what the big and little hands do, we run away with our own interpretation about how time passes.

Basically, time as a child moved pretty slowly. Christmas would never get here and we would never grow up and get our own place away from rule-making parents. The older you get, however, the big and little hands whirl around with dizzying speed. Weekends run fast, workweeks run slow. Alarm clocks are abusive and clock timers that remind you to do something seem harassing. Then, twice a year there's a marathon Sunday morning to reset them all, if you remember how to do it.

My daughter vented about her husband the other day over a disagreement about being on time. He was coming in after planting and asked that she pick him up at a certain location at the edge of the field. He obsessed about the exact time so that his transition from tractor to car would be perfectly efficient in his busy schedule.

"How about 7:15?" he requested. "No," he rethought, "better 7:13 and 20 seconds so I won't have to wait long."

After dropping laundry and dinner preparations, she left at 7:05 and arrived at the appointed location at exactly 7:12 complete with baby in car seat. Then she sat in the middle of nowhere, said ho-hum a few times and watched the sunset. The baby grew fussy as it got dark outside. Forty five minutes later he arrived with, "oh, whoops, I guess I ran a bit late."

She didn't let him forget that for several days with, "…and when YOU need something on time, then I have to drop everything, but when I…"

When it comes to reading clocks, however, my daughter wins no prizes, either. Her high school homeroom got so used to her being late that on one rare occasion when she was on time, the whole class stood and cheered. I guess she said "later, mom" so often that she figured the hands on the clock didn't move until she decided she was ready. If it were about helping with the dishes, the clock stood still.

She missed a funeral and nearly a wedding because she couldn't get somewhere on time. And that was before her boys were born, giving her credit now for the fact that young children slow the process a bit. She breezes in the door at her workplace two minutes before start time – maybe two minutes after -- with practically a toothbrush in one hand and hair brush in the other. If she has a whole two minutes left over, she thinks that she has time to run out to put gas in the tank.

She comes by her somewhat dysfunctional concept of time quite honestly. Her dad used to careen into the work parking lot on two wheels, screech to a halt and wonder why the entire staff was outside glaring at him. He does the same screeching, two-wheeled style arriving late at weddings, funerals and all other events that clearly post a start time.

I gave my daughter an over-sized clock for her kitchen this past Christmas. Maybe there's hope that the next generation can tell time.

# Laughing Just For Giggles

I recently met someone whose sense of humor resembled that of a corpse. Maybe he was laughing on the inside, but on the outside his face registered zero on the Richter scale. I got the feeling that if he actually cracked a smile that he would bleed to death.

When he stiffly strode away with the body language of a mannequin, I tried desperately to imagine what this person does for entertainment or...a few laughs.

Maybe he looks for typos in the phone directory for general day-to-day amusement. Or, perhaps he pours over casket catalogs to unwind after work. I wonder if arranging the coat hangers to point the same direction is high on his list of priorities in life.

I also wondered what someone who doesn't laugh thinks about. I imagined that he would speculate that two or more persons per square yard at the work place laughing together indicates that there is a huge waste of time going on. In fact, he probably can't wait to rush to his calculator to figure the negative impact upon the Gross National Product of four laughing people.

And his reading preferences? Does he enjoy a nice thick insurance policy on a rainy day, or does he like lighter fare – the fine print on an aspirin bottle, for instance?

And, for an evening's outing, I imagine that he and a few scowling friends get together for a round of cod liver oil and discuss whether or not they should push for legislation that eradicated all laughter from public places. The punishment would vary with the intensity of the crime. A mere smile would cost a hefty fine, while the louder the laugh all the way up to a huge guffaw would cost jail time for the humored offender.

117

Then with order restored, to his delight, everyone would march around with mean looks and not waste time laughing.

The fact is, the less people laugh, the more I laugh at them. There is something about all that seriousness that they must control that makes me want to burst their deadpan bubble. It's only life, after all, and none of us gets out of it alive.

I always thought that laughter was a human condition of health. As children, we did it naturally. All it took was my grandmother's serious jowls or my uncle's ill-fitting pants that hung sideways. My cousin and I used to peer through an upstairs open register and laugh at the mere sight of boring grownups sitting like still life in the living room below.

"Ahem," some boring grownup would say.

"Honk!" someone else would blow into a handkerchief.

Then my grandmother would clear her throat and say four words. Three other people would cup their ears and say, "What?" and she would have to repeat it several times.

"Oh. Mmm." The response, then rocking chairs would squeak.

So, of course, we imitated the above "conversation" complete with the longest faces we could muster up.

As a child, I think I perfected the technique of always laughing at adult misfortune. My favorite memory was when my cousin was unhappy about some disciplinary measure handed down by her dad. She slammed the door so hard that the glass shattered into a thousand pieces. My uncle was not amused. I still laugh at that image of his hostile look behind that falling glass.

Or the time that my mother couldn't see through an icy windshield, so she drove with her head out the window and yelled at me to shut up at the same time.

In grade school, of course, we always laughed at anything slightly out of order in the classroom. One stray hiccup, and we were out of control.

Then I hemorrhaged my way through high school with a few friends by perfecting the art of laughing silently. That way, we could devote the entire class hour to vibrating behind a Kleenex while appearing completely normal. And once again, anything out of order or an unfortunate moment

118

about someone else would trigger laughter.

That included straight-laced Latin teacher Miss Haswell whose shoes squeaked, the math teacher who couldn't solve her own problem and the way another classmate sneezed in three syllables.

So, to all of you scowling frumps who don't laugh at everything – ha ha, I do it at you.

# Leaping Into 'Feb-you-Wary'

The Romans must have been clinically depressed when they added the month of February to the calendar. It arrives today as the dysfunctional non-chapter of the year that is long on dullness and short on time.

We've shaken ourselves loose from the holidays and are ready for action. But there's no action. Just more of the same. It's Mother Nature's way of telling us that we have to cool our heels and pace a while longer. Maybe do a cabin fever dance while looking out the window.

The bills fly in at lightening speed with immediate due dates. The measly 28 days doled out in a non-leap year are jammed from blue Monday to blue Monday without any grace period for "minimum payment due" or "please remit now." With a straightjacket around the checkbook, there is little financial wiggle room for some shopping to perhaps lift our spirits.

It can be argued that January is equally as depressing. But some hermit time is deserved following holiday hoopla. January can be viewed as rehab time to clean, organize and attempt New Year's resolutions, even if the world seems a wintry black and white outside the window.

And besides that, you can pronounce, "January." There's not an English professor alive who can articulate February as anything but, "Feb-you-wary." So all that grade school memorizing of the correct placement of r's was a waste of time. In Feb-you-wary, it is a time to slant through the day feeling neither uprightly energized nor downrightly peaceful. It's time to pace and wish for March, Ides and all.

I am further unconvinced that Valentine's Day counts as a holiday to look forward to. On or about that date, there were Biblical martyrs, a timely massacre and birds that mated in the Middle Ages. The greeting card industry wants us to observe these blessed events by filling the aisles with gushy displays of hearts and flowers five minutes after the New Year. Try as the create-a-holiday industry might, it still does not make me forget being burned by not receiving a Valentine card from the cute boy in fifth grade.

Once February arrives, it's also time to start something about taxes, the ultimate reality event. Or at least transfer the official forms from mail box to dining room table. From there you procrastinate. After all, there's six whole weeks before due date unless, of course, you entertain at Easter. Then the procrastinated tax stuff goes from dining room table to elsewhere and perhaps out of sight, out of mind.

But back to February. It can snowstorm, ice storm, rainstorm or mood storm. All my problems, I rationalize, would be solved if I could just go out in the garden. But I have to stay inside longer.

I even think that Mother Nature is depressed with wild mood swings. A fluke of unusual weather in February might produce a warm front. The perennials and flowering trees are fooled into thinking it is spring. But oops! Back underground, here comes another cold front.

My house is even depressed in February. The curtains are suddenly crooked and I am sick to death of them. The houseplants are dropping leaves, wishing for longer days. The furnace huffs and puffs and wants a new filter and the cats don't like their new litter on sale. All the unfinished projects are glaring at me. The walls seem to have new cracks and the stairs creak even more. The basement glares at me for more order and fewer spider webs.

I'm with the Romans. If the month of February must remain, then I'll be just as clinically depressed during leap year as any other.

# Liar, Liar, Pants on Fire!

I had to take out my driver's license the other day and happened to notice that the identification weight was 50 pounds less than the truth.

For the moment, I thought I'd make a joke out of it. But then maybe the checker would wonder who I really was – the anorexic shadow of my former self or a wannabe runway model for Hags Magazine. After all, the birth date matched the number of chins and gray hair, so I pretended to be the oldest living pregnant hag and kept my mouth shut.

I guess that makes me a liar. Maybe just a little white liar.

Ordinarily, I just can't haul off a little white lie like some people, let alone the major whoppers told to the press by murderers, performance drug takers and greedy corporations.

It should have been an early warning when I cheated on a spelling test in the fifth grade and burst into tears when the teacher caught me. I was mortified and had to stay inside for recess.

But later in high school, stern Latin teacher Miss Haswell left the room while we took a vocabulary test. Maybe a mood to rebel swept the class because we all openly discussed our test answers until she returned.

I was later overcome by guilt, however, and 'fessed up. She was glad that I was "woman enough" to admit to my cheating and made me take the test over. Ever since Miss Haswell's jowls chastised me, I have become the world's worst liar.

If I tell someone I dislike that I am happy to see him, my voice falters. If I were to take a lie detector test about how many chocolate cookies I had at a holiday gathering, the needle would register 8.9 on the Richter scale. I once told a friend caller that I was just on my way out the door, when really I just didn't want to listen to how he knew everything. At, "on my way out the door," my voice crackled and I blushed so hard that the phone steamed at his end.

I was never even good at lying to my small children when "later," really meant "never." They caught on fast, though, and made sure that I had a written promise, signed and sealed by Notary Public that yes, we would go get ice cream "later." I just never quite defined "later." But it wasn't a lie if ever in our lives we went for ice cream.

Lying about age has always been fashionable, especially with women. I never did that too much unless, of course, you count the times when you were asked your age at the door of a pub. I did that once in New York City when I was just under the legal age of 18. The bouncer nodded me in as I tried to look more sophisticated than my zit-infested complexion.

I can't even lie on my taxes. If my accountant tells me to deduct mileage when going to and from the office supply store, I will dutifully note that I snuck in the grocery store on the way because I needed to pick up some calcium and anti-wrinkle cream.

These days, there's nothing really to lie about. I don't care how old I am or how I look. I am not trying to impress anyone with some sort of mystique that elevates me to something that I'm not.

But I'm still not going to change the weight on my driver's license.

# Coming Clean on the Laundry

You can tell a lot about people by how they do their laundry. I have come to learn that there are as many styles of laundry-keeping out there as there are personality types.

The Type A person who must fold the towels "just so" and then counsel members of the family to do the same are completely out of my social circle. In fact, after becoming aware that there are towel folders like this, I have adopted a new policy when meeting people for the first time. Right after, "Hello, how are you?" I ask if they care how their towels are folded. If they go into geometric instructions with visual aids and handout sheets, they're off my list immediately.

But what a dull world if everyone simply marched to the same rinse cycle by collecting dirty clothes in a basket and processing from wash to dryer without personal style.

I admit that I am weak about the putting-the-clothes-away stage. It is unintentional, but nevertheless a fact that when daily life is a one-woman show, doing laundry often ends at the bottom of the priority list. That means that when I get out of the shower, the clean towels and next set of clothes are often conveniently two floors down and still in the dryer.

I obviously have slipped a little with laundry discipline since having a child or two around the house. My daughter used to leave her wet clothes in the washer until mildew set in, then transferred them to the dryer for several days until the wrinkles were well established. I spent much time trying to make an appointment to do my own laundry.

My other excuse is that I was well-trained by once living in a house that had a laundry chute from the second floor. That means, besides small children hurling toys and peanut butter sandwiches to the basement, the dirty clothes fell by gravity quite easily. A bit too easily, in fact, because then it seemed a great labor to get them back up to the second floor. It was sort of like throwing yourself down a steep sand dune, then huffing and puffing your way back up.

About having the clean clothes still in the basement, I was one-upped by a male who admitted that his were still stacked in his truck in the driveway because he couldn't seem to get them back inside after the Laundromat event. So he dressed for work while on the way to work.

That beats another male acquaintance who simply hung his clean pants on the back door knob to save time from finding them elsewhere. And here I thought every male, while living in an unassisted care facility (himself without female supervision) simply didn't do laundry and bought new underwear every time he ran out. I think that my husband had about 89 pairs of Jockey shorts by the time we married.

I was corrected the other day, however, by another male who keeps up his laundry quite well, but has altered his standards of clean. In the days when his mother did his laundry, he said, "one wrinkle and it went into the basket." Now, having to do it himself, he decides that maybe only one mustard stain, as opposed to two, will pass for clean.

My favorite dig against my ex-husband came about when he questioned that perhaps our daughter at age 11 was too young to do her own laundry. I suddenly remembered that he had shipped in his mother to do his laundry when I moved out.

The moment was too good and I couldn't pass it up as I prepared my forked tongue. "And how old should one be to push two buttons, though I realize that 47 is still too young?"

He never mentioned laundry again. His mother has now gone to laundry heaven, probably folding her towels, "just so." I understand that he currently drives through an all-service cleaners and stuffs his bag through a window. They take everything from Levi's to Jockey shorts. I guess that beats buying new underwear every week.

# Literature of the Third Age

They are saying that our reading habits are becoming nonexistent these days, or "the dumbing down of America," as one writer summed it up.

Actually, the volume of reading hasn't changed, only the subject matter. I remember a time when I kept a classic book authored by one of the Bronte sisters by my bedside, or carried a powerful best seller in my bag wherever I went.

But now I carry around directions in fine print. That would be directions for child car seat assembly, directions for the operation of a new digital gismo and directions about how to remove directions from the shipping box.

The book of directions that accompany every product sold today usually is as thick as an Old World dictionary. There are at least 18 languages, including Swahili and Toddlerese. Once you thumb through the pages and finally find English about how to safely operate your new toaster/calcucamera, time is up and you must do something else.

Then the warrantee, too tedious to read, says in another 30 thick paragraphs that the enclosed product promises to work until it doesn't, then it's the purchaser's tough luck and no fault of the manufacturers so therefore don't bother them with your petty complaints (Bronx cheer).

Someone gave me a cute little digital gadget that can record brief thoughts or a grocery list while on the road. Once I got past the unpacking stage, I unfolded ten square feet of directions for a palm-sized recorder. I recorded two "things to do" and one belch from someone in the room and the thing blinked "FULL" for three weeks. I decided then that I had better take the standard advice, "when in doubt, read the directions."

But, since I work for a living, there was no time.  I was already behind in my reading list because there was a library of other directions to digest. I had yet to assemble a hummingbird feeder and a figure out how to record a new greeting on the answering machine after a brief storm outage.

Luckily, I had to have a new car muffler installed, so I could spend time in the shop reading directions and becoming an expert on steps A through D.

There's just way too much information for every product!  Most of the time, we don't utilize half of the features that we could on these products. My computer is probably programmed to brew coffee and blow kisses if I really pursued the "Help" menu enough.  But I'm too busy reading the information about the new cat box.  After that, my goal in life is to read the instructions for a windup toy for my grandson.

Then a work friend sold me a perfectly good used printer for ten dollars. I was thrilled about the price, so I took a chance about not having the setup directions, for a change.  That was several months ago and my computer is still hostile to that low-class printer that came without directions.

Even the food ingredients are a major reading project.  I've decided that if the paragraph is too long with words that end with too many suffixes that make it sound like the syllabus of a college chemistry class, then I won't buy it.  It must not be real food, I justify but, really, I just don't have time to read it.

It gets down to bananas, the only sacred thing left to buy without paperwork.

I would not have time to read about bananas, anyway, because I'm too busy reading my bedside version of "How to set your new alarm clock."

# Making Noise About Men

I try not to jump on the male versus female food fight too often these days. Some gender will always accuse me of some bashing or another. I always hear from all those testosterone-infected, belching and scratching – er, I mean nice men out there.

Sometimes I can't resist, however. It seems that all those chauvinistic divisions are just too amusing to ignore with all the Moons and Venuses apart that we seem to be at times.

Especially for us divorced, widowed or just plain peace-and-quiet-seeking women who exist outside the noisy realm of men. And I do mean noisy.

I've experienced both sides of the noise line now. When incarcerated within a happy-thwappy marriage, my most vivid recollection is about a male's dominating decibels. My husband cranked up the stereo in the basement family room so that I, two floors away, could not hear myself knit.

If I shouted through the laundry chute to turn it down, of course he couldn't hear. So I had to personally visit the basement to perform sign language, known as Wrathful Gestures.

But in reverse, if I were in the bathtub with the water running and HE wanted my attention, I was expected to dash toweled and dripping wet to HIS area; thus the saying, "You know I can't hear you with the water running."

I think that his goal was to get the speakers to walk unassisted across the room. Noise was his statement about what he was doing at the moment and how he felt about it. Open, slam, open, slam of the kitchen cupboards meant that he was disturbed about my activities that day and dinner wasn't on the table. Rattle, chink, clink in upper case letters meant, "I'm the only one who does the trash around here."

129

When we socialized with friends, the stereo in the same room was blasting so that conversation with the person next to you was impossible.

I questioned this, having to shout, "How are you?" to someone next to me. His answer was that the music was more important. "Then why invite them over?" fell on deaf ears.

Then, of course, there's the snoring issue. Your average steam ship comes to mind. While I am gently informed by family members that I, too, snore these days, "That's different," is my response, just like his "that's different" in any other verbal exchange.

My snoring is gentle, pinked-ruffled rhythms of sweetness and light. Some males sound like a monstrous Mr. Snuffleuffagus shaking the countryside.

When not cranking up the stereo or snoring, my husband thrived on engine revs in the driveway. These events were not for a simple auto-repair test, but to irritate every neighbor on the block, except other like-minded males who joined him in appreciation for all things that rev.

They bonded over every high-octane sputter. I'm sure that they all grew up making armpit noises in church.

Other fascinating noises include the speed of the fan that must make as much noise as possible. They, too, should walk across the room. If a summer day calls for gentle air movement, my husband thought that the noisiest speed was in order.

In the car, windows flew up and down, sky roofs opened and closed and the radio settled between stations on the loudest static.

I don't understand it. When I travel with a female, we adjust the air at a gentle speed and calmly converse in peace and quiet.

His noisy past came back to shout at him, though. A friend said the other day that he cupped his ear in her direction. It seems that he now needs a hearing aid.

"What?" he said.

# MiNdiNg tHe 'MeNtoſS' FſoM My DiSciPLiNe Square

I recently noticed the word "mentor" used on an office-related program.

It was included in a program where one department of assorted clerical suspects comes to visit total strangers in another department to inform those who have performed their jobs for 20 years how to perform those jobs.

The so-named mentors would then instruct the seasoned workers about "discipline squares." The painted square defines exactly where a trash barrel, parts bin, a worker's lunch and Kleenex in one's purse belong. Venturing outside of that discipline square means that someone at corporate level loses sleep.

And then since I am left-handed and may put the trash bin in a slightly different location, I personally disturb the Gross National Product, which should be at about zero now with everyone standing around doing nothing in discipline squares.

This is apparently a new wave of the style of manufacturing in this country to compete on a global scale. Upper management of Fortune 500 companies that buy each other and get larger cannot seem to find out information any other way. (Isn't this the computer age?) So if the workers do nothing and stand saluting in the same spot, nothing is produced. But that's good because then management knows that nothing is going on and, therefore, there is no information or production to manage. Then, with any luck, they can conveniently close that particular plant because nothing is going on. It makes corporate life a lot easier.

At least that's what the "mentors" freed from their cubicles seemed enthusiastic about as they busily planned discipline squares on the floor.

Maybe I respect the English language too much, but to me the word "mentor" belongs somewhere up there with word royalty. It should be used sparingly, say one per life span. It has no place on office memos or petty programs. One does not sign up to be a mentor.

To me, a mentor is that one person who has a profound and lasting voice in your training that enriches your working knowledge of a profession or activity. It might be the fifth grade teacher who recognized something and encouraged you with just the right words at just the right time. And you'll never forget her.

Or, it might be an outstanding tool and die man who monitored your precision 25 years ago, who scoffed at your mistakes, who accepted your correctness and left an indelible mark on your work thereafter.

Or, it might be come from the pages of some writer that you've never met, but whose work you refer to forever as your model and mentor.

It might be the church figure that helped and counseled you through rough times. Whomever your mentor, he or she has a silent and everlasting voice over your shoulder.

My handy-dandy American Heritage College Dictionary, in fact, defines mentor as "a wise and trusted counselor or teacher."

So if anyone occupying an ordinary office function can sign up to be a mentor for an hour to plan discipline squares, then a two-bit Hot Flashes columnist can sign up to be a best-selling writer of The Third Age.

And as highly-revered American authoress, I can sign up to be a famous authority on outspoken behavior in public places. Then I can do a literary tour to give inspirational lectures on how to effectively write useless articles that prove nothing.

And, while I have signed up to pretend that I am famous, I can sign up to live a famous lifestyle. With an up-scale house somewhere peaceful with acres of gardens and a comfy loft where the computer/library is and a beamed ceiling kitchen and stained glass everywhere leading to the cathedral ceiling living room.

And when I sign up to be important, then I'll stop chewing my nails so that I can have something constructive to do while I manicure them, sip my wine out of crystal stems and read classics other than my own.

Then, since I have signed up to be important I can also approach total strangers elsewhere to inform them how they should live. For instance, I should march into corporate level meetings at Fortune 500 companies to plan discipline squares for them.

I would explain, with an air of authority, how they must move, where they must locate their laptops and what location in the "situation room" that they may use.

But before I become that kind of a mentor, I'll be in my discipline square for a while doing nothing.

# Death By Chocolate

had occasion to visit the doctor for some checkup or another recently and was weighed, blood pressured and otherwise given the boring once over.

Oddly enough, my blood pressure numbers were good, though I confessed to an entire pot of coffee that morning along with checking the world news and assessing my disastrous household after a visit from young grandsons the day before.

"Any unusual depressive episodes within the last month?" the nurse asked. Other than arguing with my daughter about life in general? Well, I still work for a living if that's any indication that my mental health is at risk. I didn't mention that the mere sight of my lunch box caused nervous reaction, or that my car shuddered at the sight of the work parking lot. Nor did I reveal that I would probably enter the work place with a pink weapon laced with needlepoint and promptly threaten everyone within 20 feet that questioned my crossword puzzle underneath work papers.

I also forgot to mention teensy details like working alongside a drug addict on a forklift one day and nearly run over by another the next. Normal people on the outside who work in normal places probably wouldn't believe me.

"Do you do tobacco or alcohol?" she looked over her glasses. I wish. I might go back to smoking if the workplace continues. And everyone knows that you must drink alcohol regularly if you are employed this week and about to be unemployed next.

"Any other abuses?" Well, I have been hitting the chocolate heavily lately which explains about three pounds gained since last time. She let that one go.

"You don't understand," and I went on to explain that my health habits are normally stellar with fresh vegetables, very little fat and plenty of designer water from day to day. I added that I also walk a mile regularly. She wondered what was wrong with a little chocolate here and there.

Well, I went on, the workplace has a candy machine handy with those Reese's butter cups reaching out to me at a minor fortune of change for three of them to get me through the next hour or so. There's a magnet on the Reese's slot that pulls my change pocket from door to machine. I have no choice but to put the coins in. Then, the next time I feel sorry for myself – about two hours later – the Reese's slot attacks me again. I figure that it's a slow suicide by chocolate as long as I work for a living with candy machines all around.

She suggested to save money that I buy the Reese's butter cups at a regular store and not spend so much at the machine. "But," I explained, "I shouldn't eat chocolate so I don't buy them at the store. She gave up. She noticed that my health didn't seem to be in jeopardy from a little chocolate here and there.

Yeah, well lots of chocolate here and there.

Then she noticed the zits. Was I allergic and to what? Well, chocolate. Her computer imploded and I was convinced that Reese's butter cups spun around the room. I'm serious, I told her, I just can't control the chocolate when at the workplace.

She asked me how long I would be working. I gave her the date and said that I might be dead by then from chocolate, fat and zits. She laughed and doubted it, but then didn't realize that a hag friend had already asked why there was a new candy machine in my front room.

# Mother Nature's Biggest Blunder Yet

**M**other Nature seems to have restless moods of ups and downs. Sometimes She casts a green spell of peace, other times She is on the warpath. She does snowstorms, flooding, earthquakes and tornadoes at the drop of a hat. There are spells when we are just thankful for a calm day on this planet when it doesn't jiggle, flood or turn into a frowning funnel.

And with earthly unrest all over, She is getting hotter yet. Her fever is rising, and we had better take note.

But as disease and pestilence have shaped our past thanks to Mother Nature, there are now new and even more dangerous threats in the future to reckon with: Black Pod, Witches Broom and Frosty Pod Rot. The occurrence of these plant diseases might just throw us all into the worst frenzy of disorder yet. They might even top the Bubonic Plague or Spanish Influenza in their impact on the world population.

That is because these plant disorders are attacking the cacao seed. In plain English, it means that our chocolate supply is endangered and thus causing a possible shortage! (We will now pause to clutch our throats.)

I mentioned this to a friend the other day and she suddenly remembered that her regular supply of dark chocolate was suspiciously off the shelves at the grocery store. "Black Pod, Witches Broom and Frosty Pod Rot will be the end of life as we know it," I warned her with an ominous finger raised.

She began shaking. Certainly, I was kidding, she thought. But no, I showed her the article in a newspaper. It was a brief report, unassuming and probably written without any forethought about the importance of chocolate in this world. When I first read it, my eyes bulged sensing impending doom and distress at where these cacao diseases may lead.

In fact, I ran to see if my supply of mint chocolate chips were still around. I put them in the freezer for future emergencies. I considered a storm cellar for a private stash.

The first thing that will occur is that the dwindling number of countries that grows disease-free cacao seed will be forced to raise prices to exorbitant rates. One Hershey's bar will require mortgaging the house. As the chocolate shortage mounts, so will world tensions. Thus the chocolate wars begin.

Then PMS insurgents will establish cells all over the world. They're against all those wasteful chocolate imbibers who refuse to share their stores of semi-sweet dark bars. Hormonal warrior women will invade those countries still untouched by the disease Witches Brooms to attempt a chocolate legislature.

To no one's surprise, those legislatures will function only on days when Reese's Pieces are available.

The defending Hershey's troops, fueled by rations of home-made chocolate chip cookies, will try to defend the pod fields. But alas, a shortage of Oreos will take down their supplies of proper sustenance.

The rest of the civilized world will attempt to fashion a chocolate substitute. Skeptics will come out of the woodwork to assess the properties of synthetic chocolate. If it doesn't cause zits, alleviate PMS or increase weight, then it's back to the drawing board.

Meantime, all this chocolate turmoil will cause more hormone wars – the PMSers against the Hot Flashers -- the factions that need more chocolate. If the earth doesn't perish in all this turmoil, then maybe all of humanity will adjust to the reality of the extinction of cacao pod seeds.

A world without chocolate is hard to imagine, though.

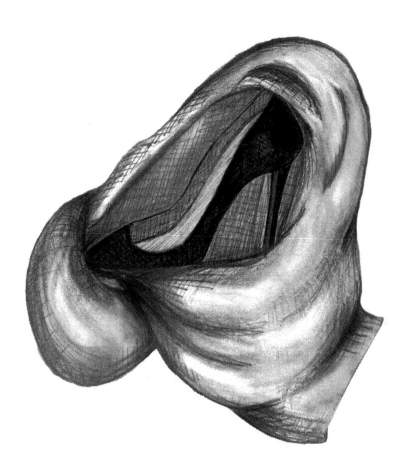

# BeWare tHe WratH oF HurricaNe Hag

The storm experts say that hurricane season lasts some six months. It's always a busy spell as the likes of feminine names and proper males line up out there to slam the coasts.

If I were on the official committee to name hurricanes in their alphabetical order, I would have stopped at the H's. Something about Hurricane Hag might be the most fearful. Never mind the distinguished Gustav, then the youthful Hanna. When Hurricane Hag hits, there'll be historic revelations about the wrath of stormy women.

Right now she may be spinning out there as a mere tropical depression. That means that she is depressed about being hot. She fans her hot flashes, but gradually builds steam each day that she takes on more menopausal crises, more mid-section fat and deepening wrinkles.

Day and night, she may be weaving her way in her growing depression, cranking out her daily life and meandering in a thankless direction. She spins her moods here and there. In her tropical depression, she worries that she'll never work up her winds to make a difference in her life.

But wait. An arrogant male hurricane has been reported to cross her path. He is one of those die-hard early alphabetically named hurricanes. He didn't quite succumb before the H's and certainly didn't see what was coming. He is still vying for top hurri-canine. He could be Hurricane Belch, Hurricane Ego, Hurricane Ex-husband or maybe Hurricane Co-worker Who Thinks He is Superior to Hurricane Hag.

Hurricane Hag is gathering forces now and has escalated to a Category Two hurricane, or "Cat 2," as they slickly say in the news cycle hurricane biz. In her Cat 2 winds, she works up froth and increases her speed. She promises to be fearful and make Hurricane Cocky look like a wimpy wisp.

Meantime, she had to be sure that she was swirling straight. Was that Hurricane Ego that just scoffed at her 90 mph winds? Did he actually think that she was a minor storm and would never be strong enough or organized enough to amount to anything but a blip on the screen?

Hardly. Hurricane Hag is ready, able and storming. And she has tornado and tsunami witnesses that verified she is coming, and coming strong.

While Hurricane Hag whirls herself into a heightening storm, she takes on fierce winds that are fueled by the warm climate with chocolate, caffeine and expensive wine. Her wrath is increasing with her waistline. She is a sure storm to watch because she doesn't care about anyone in her menopausal path, especially arrogant hurricanes.

She is projected to arrive everywhere as soon as Hurricane Cocky, with his empty huff and puff, leaves the area. By then, she'll be listed as one of the most dangerous storms ever. Never mind down-grading her to a more polite female hurricane; she's hot with winds that will take any Hurricane Ego above Cat 4 and beyond.

The eye of her storm briefly calms because she knows that there's nothing more full of hot air than an arrogant hurricane who thinks that he can take over the area and scare her off. It seems that male storms have tough-fisted testosterone these days that threaten a big ordeal, but hardly pull it off. Dodging the bullet is what it's called because huff and puff winds that go nowhere, or crying wolf, are what an arrogant hurricane delivers.

But right now, she's just spinning her depression somewhere out there. Watch out for the wrath of Hurricane Hag when she is crossed by Hurricane Ego!

# NaMe-DroppINg THat GoeS 'THUd'

I t's rather the sound of brain cells falling to the ground along with the names of everyone that you ever knew.

Not to be confused with real name-dropping, of course, which refers to one who casually works a famous name into the conversation so as to impress others. "As I mentioned the issue to the Pope the other day..."

I hardly qualify as a name-dropper since I have never brushed with fame. Unless an episode with premier dancer Rudoph Nureyev in the '70s counts. To me, it was the high point of my whole life to study his derriere, hip rotation and calf muscles from a mere two feet away in the ballet studio. If I had reached out, I could have touched his sweat!

"Who again, Sue?" And by the time I explain who Nureyev was, everyone yawns. Once, when I lived in an apartment over a liquor store, Cassius Clay, in the days before he became Mohammad Ali, stood across the street gathering a small crowd. Had I been slightly clever, I could have shouted something so that I could name-drop the next day. "And Cassius told me the other day..."

But dropping a name that goes thud is another matter. It's when you cannot remember for the life of you the name of the person you just met. I remember if the guy was cute or the woman was disgustingly thin, but not the name.

I know someone who can work a room like putty. She sweeps around and remembers names, life stories and family scandals. Then she would say to me out of the side of her mouth, "remind me to tell you later about her closet skeleton and who her real father was and why the cow jumped over the moon..."

Forgetting children's names is legal. My grandmother went through two aunts and a cousin before she got to my name. I try my two children before I get to my grandsons. Sometimes there's a dog's name thrown in. They used to laugh at me until I caught my ex-husband saying "Pi-Ja, Rover, I mean Calvin." It runs in the next generation because on a recent visit, my grandson said "Grandpa, I mean Grandma..."

About name-dropping that goes thud, it's most embarrassing to walk into a store and hear a cheerful, "Hi, Sue!" when you can't remember the person's name. I respond with upbeat conversation and try to keep talking about my life history to rattle some memory cells. One solution if you still can't remember is to ask how to spell the last name to have them in your address book. I did that once, and the answer was a deadpan, "S-m-i-t-h."

Sometimes we substitute catch words that describe the person. It's easier that way when everyone in the workplace knows who "The Marlboro Man," "Bonehead" or "Dusseldorf" is. "Crabgrass" is the glaring neighbor with perfect sod and "Maybelline" wears red lipstick to empty her trash.

This habit, however, can become socially dangerous because a friend of mine was afraid that she would introduce "Hamster Woman" to "Big Foot."

One teacher friend was especially helpless about names in class so he reduced most everyone to a standard "sweetie" or "lad." Occasionally he would remember where the student was from and label by location. I never did learn the name of one student except that "St. Louis" was always late to class. Another one, he referred to as "Baby Girl," but never mentioned that the name was his favorite horse.

So whoever you are, I'll remember you by weight and looks as my brain cells fall thud.

# Not a Frequent Flyer

D on't get me wrong, there's nothing wrong with flying these days. Millions of people do it calmly and routinely everyday and don't even flinch at the thought of catapulting into a skyscraper building.

Statistics show, in fact, that it is safer to be in the air than on the ground.

Due to a certain ex-spouse, however, it is probably unsafe to be anywhere. He is likely the only one in the world who should be ticketed for tail-gating single-engine airplanes in the sky.

I should have noticed something awry about his personality when I first met him decades ago. He had an intensity about him that caused the wallpaper to unravel when he entered a room.

His heart rate is probably triple that of normal people, his blood pressure runs amuck and arms gesture constantly. He sweats when completely at rest. The only hobbies that interest him are the ones that bring him closest to death. Watching events does not interest him; he must experience anything that promises death-defying risk, preferably at several thousand feet.

Thus, he rapidly progressed from souped up Mustangs in the garage to Piper Cubs in the sky. He probably holds the record for the fastest solo pilot licensing, mainly because the instructor feared for his own life.

At that time, he had also made a wise investment in some grounded Navy trainer. You never know, after all, when you might need to have a worthless flying machine around that is only capable of taxiing noisily from one grassy location to another about 40 feet away.

But he was going to rebuild it to fly again, he claimed. He also believed that the plane was the perfect solution for eliminating city traffic. He conveniently forgot that most of his destinations – his job and hardware stores – had no runways available. Neither did we at our house in the suburbs.

My theory is that his ulterior motive was to eliminate his wife and children in one easy step. There were harrowing episodes to prove it. Like the time that we visited friends in the next state one fine winter day. After he spent the entire afternoon intensely studying weather maps (don't we all do that on social occasions?), it was determined that we should beat an ice storm back home.

That was the first time my life passed before me. It should have been the last, because I noticed that he was enormously invigorated by the blur of dials and beeps with gongs that warned of impending doom. He was having fun! Cold, dark Lake Michigan was beneath one wing, and the citified checkerboard was beneath the other. Ice threatened to form, my first born was in peril, and this is sport?

On another occasion, we gathered with friends on a Sunday. The other husband was also a single-engine pilot – birds of a feather, stick together. They puffed up their chests and packed the conversation full of VFR and IFR jargon. Once thoroughly inflated with flying testosterone, they couldn't resist going to the local airport, "just to take the boys to the watch the planes," they said, with halos over their heads.

Our parting request was to not take the children up. It was futile, however, because four floating Cheshire cat grins returned, thoroughly elated and lousy liars.

The next infamous flight was for vacation. I wondered on that take-off why I would agree to be in the air with the same man who drove through the city with murderous intentions against traffic. My baby daughter was in her last ruffles, I thought.

The highlight of that windy landing was the sight of those pink ruffled rubber pants being chased across the runway by this wild man waving his arms about. The return trip was thick fog, and again he was invigorated by challenges of near disaster and blind landings.

Sure, I fly the big ones sometimes. But I watch the captain suspiciously. If he wears a beard, gestures wildly and looks like he wants to get rid of his wife and children, I stay on the ground.

# Diet For an Old Hag

A friend nervously picked off the sesame seeds from a bun recently during an outdoor cookout.

I told her that I was not intentionally trying to poison her at this time. Then she rattled off a list of things that bother her digestion these days.

Another friend literally hung up on me long distance because of an emergency trip to the bathroom. She apologized later, but it seems that she had forgotten that some food or another makes her ill these days. Then she rattled off her list of foods that she must avoid.

Three days in a row last week, I enjoyed innocent fruit for a snack. On the fourth day, I enjoyed Kaopectate.

I guess that for some of us old hags, the days of the cast iron stomach are over. I used to gorge down pizza topped with everything but the kitchen sink with a generous sprinkling of carpenter's nails on top. Then I would slurp it down with any liquid available.

Completely invigorated, I would leap from the table, do a few cartwheels out the door and head for ballet class and rehearsal that demanded the power and energy of a football player.

Sure, I ate healthy foods, too, but it never occurred to me that I had to worry about consequences later for minor morsel offenses. Let alone, bore my friends with the complete list of what I cannot eat anymore.

I have therefore devised a diet that most of us can handle these days, and thus spend valuable conversation time on more important matters in life, like anti-wrinkle creams.

First of all, you must eliminate all onions and garlic from the premises. If this is too painful, then replace them with interesting kitchen artwork – say, charming ceramic wall art or a still life photo on the refrigerator.

149

Coffee in the morning will be replaced by boiling hot water, designer of course, and perhaps a dash of brown or tan food coloring to suit your taste. Breakfast consists of oatmeal with a sprinkling of sawdust on top, one yolkless, whiteless poached egg and a molecule of orange juice. Naturally, juice is considered wild behavior if there is sensitivity to acid, so imbibe at your own risk.

Eliminate all crunchy, munchie snacks. Anything that you ever enjoyed chewing on in your entire life is now a distant memory.

For lunch, you may have incinerated vegetables of any kind, being cautious about the Brussels sprouts family which you never liked, anyway, pulverized rice and a slice of cardboard with nothing on it. Limit yourself to ice water with a slice of lemon in it, unless, of course, the acid is offensive blah blah blah.

For dinner, chicken breasts must be boned, skinned, beaten to death, thrown against the wall and cremated before serving on a plate with smashed potatoes with a mere illusion of butter on top and, again, your choice of incinerated vegetable. The salad consists of sliced cucumbers that must have the skin and seeds removed until pared down to the size of a straw, celery with the strings removed until there is nothing, imaginary lettuce and no-acid tomatoes topped with no dressing.

Dessert is a luscious photograph of whatever you once enjoyed.

Water intake must be drastically reduced, and consumed only at home with a completely open schedule to make bathroom trips every five minutes. No water must be taken after dinner.

You must also carry a whole pharmacy of stomach remedies at all times. That way, if you have scheduled the exact moment that something digests improperly, then you'll have some sort of relief before you reach the next bathroom.

The diet for an old hag has made reading menus at restaurants a much faster activity. Since you cannot eat anything, just skim it to act socially normal, then suddenly pretend that you are not hungry.

If this new diet seems uninteresting, then the addition of a carafe of very expensive wine every day is probably in order. Then you won't care about the after-effects.

150

# "O PHONy Tree, O PHONy Tree"

I used to be a snob about having a live Christmas tree for the holidays.

Then a friend bailed out and bought an artificial tree several years ago. How low class, I thought. Where is her genuine Christmas spirit?

Why, what would Christmas be without tromping through a frozen or muddy pasture carrying murderous weapons and arguing with children about which one was most perfect? Or how spiritless to have no appropriate vehicle to transport the thing and have it sail off the top of the car at 60 mph.

Or certainly, Christmas would not be Christmas if the newly sawed tree fit perfectly in the stand, didn't fall over several times to break heirloom ornaments or failed to shed a bushel of needles down the cold air return. There's no such thing as a joyous holiday unless the vacuum cleaner clogs and breaks a belt by New Year's.

But ah, the smell of real pine, I say. "Just get some fragrant incense," they say.

I once bought a live tree from a lot, also against my holiday principles. It held the Guinness Book of Records for the most needles lost per hour that year.

Then the arguing children grew up and left. They returned a couple years to help me out with saw and truck, but then I was left on my own. I also began to worry about fire hazards since I almost had one a few years ago from an errant candle.

One year, though I had artfully decorated a six-foot ficus plant and had heirloom ornaments on a small one in the hallway, the family was miffed about having no regular tree.

"Yeah," my son grumbled, "and there's not even rum for the eggnog."

Feeling like the Grinchess, I began to rethink the artificial tree. After

151

all, they look rather charming in the store.

In the box, however, they are more like a ton of bricks. I should have forecast an unpleasant episode when it took two gorilla-sized males to hoist it into the trunk. I managed to make it across town without incident, but nearly injured myself getting it to the porch. The dog ran for cover when I approached the door dragging the coffin-sized container.

Always looking on the bright side (after all, 'tis the season), I decided the $100 container was a wise real estate investment should I need a box to live in when I am homeless and unemployed.

The next bad sign was that ominous phrase "some assembly required." The official assemblers had also grown and gone elsewhere. They always approached the assembly as a no-brainer. Others view it as a challenge, sort of like pursuing an engineering degree. I think it's torture. If I don't get it after reading the same sentence four times, I simply throw the paper in the air and leave the room in a huff.

After an entire afternoon to assemble the stand, stem and turn-style branches, I have now accomplished my first artificial tree. I don't know whether or not I am pleased. It can be shaped and reshaped by some 1,000 pipe-cleaner branches. No doubt, some grown child will march in and snicker at the color-coded layer that can still be seen through the branches.

It stands upright, but looks a bit too…cheerful. There are no flaws. I will miss the accidents, needles, clogged vacuum and the real pine scent.

There had better not be negative comments or I'll withhold the rum again.

# Occupation: Pigeon Lady

That's what my next tax form might read. That is, if I get more disgusted with what it takes to afford food, clothing, shelter and gas. My budget is evaporating into thin air faster than the poles are melting into the seas

From week to week, we working slobs haul in groceries, haul out trash and fill our tanks to get to the job so that we can afford to fill our tanks to get to the job. There's nothing left over to save for retirement and no quality time either.

The work place furthermore ensures that for every wage-earning slob there is no life left at the end of the day. It is a hard and fast rule, in fact, that is published in the employee handbook when hired.

"...and the EMPLOYEE shall agree that from here to eternity the EMPLOYER shall own and operate every bodily organ and every breathing moment of the EMPLOYEE'S existence, which includes, but is not limited to, the right for the EMPLOYER to follow the EMPLOYEE home and demand that he or she sit up straight and salute the EMPLOYER until the alarm clock goes off to report back to work."

Yes, it is a good thing to be gainfully employed, but a better balance of work versus life should be in order.

Some decades ago, the alternative was called "dropping out" from the rat race that seemed to have questionable values. So those who "dropped out" from highly charged careers in large organizations escaped to communes near the mountains with the promise to live happily and peacefully off the land. No bosses or rules, just funny smelling cigarettes.

But the very communal life that promised peaceful coexistence proved that even with unconventional lifestyles, we don't like each other there, either. While I liked the nature part of it, I never joined the circles that passed the funny smelling pipe. That was too much peace and quiet for a yakky social animal.

But I still dream on about the dropping out of the rat race, or retiring – a vanishing idea. If I were a pigeon lady, for instance, I could schedule my own time with my own rules. I could take breaks whenever and how long I want. I could take time to talk to strangers and smell the roses. There would be no competition for the job and no resume to embellish. There would be no EMPLOYER to examine my bladder contents and no interview where I must wear panty hose.

I could make ugly faces and glare, or I could prance around and act goofy. The pigeons would like me anyway.

So I pursued information about being a pigeon lady, completely forgetting, of course, the detail about making an income. The first thing I discovered was that the pigeons had been sent to Mexico. Fountains and theatres in big cities were bare as the pigeon lady force was cut to only a few hopefuls who had just completed pigeon lady certification.

The bottom line on the pigeon computer, however, failed to account for the fact that American-fed pigeons become faint in Mexico and could not subsist on a steady diet of hot peppers. Nor was it considered that the afternoon siesta occurred at the exact hour when hard working American pigeon ladies spread feed.

Pigeon feed, furthermore, was imported from China. But with no pigeons or market demand, the price escalated to be unaffordable by the pigeon ladies. They were standing in unemployment lines, anyway, bemoaning the loss of their faithful companions.

Maybe dropping out in those offbeat communes isn't such a bad idea, after all.

# Playing the Board Game Called 'Gasopoly'

It's a new game to add to your list appropriate for all driver licensees ages 16 and up. Though I suspect that we are already playing it on a daily basis. It begins at "start," and ends with no winners.

Distributed by "Hasnotbro," in conjunction with the oil companies, the board game is already creating a stir among us innocent commuters. It takes our budget on a roller coaster promising to irritate all who dare pull out of their driveway or roll the dice.

Rather than the flat iron, boot or dog, Gasopoly tokens include a car that gas-guzzles, a car that sort of gas-guzzles, a hag's car with an empty tank and a hag's car with a full tank.

At "go," the dice might lead the hag with a full tank to come upon a gas station whose price has suddenly dropped ten cents per gallon. The next roll of the dice might take the hag with an empty tank to a station where the price of gas has suddenly risen by at least 20 cents per gallon.

The gas stations around the board are suitably called "Cashgo," "Lastbuckgo" and "Shellout." Where ever you advance around the board there are pitfalls and snags to make sure that you never, ever get ahead.

The only way out is to draw a "Chance" card that says, "Advance to Community Chest, but fill your tank along the way."

The properties to land on that are most lucrative are, rather than the railroads, the oil companies, of course. That would include the Greeding Oil Company, the Racketvania Oil Company, the Gouge & Run Oil Company and the Profit Line.

But whoops! The dice never allows the player to buy because the oil companies want exclusive profits. Remember, there are no winners in this game.

The hot properties to buy are still "Boardwalk" and "Park Place," and, yes, you can still put hotels on them, but buyer beware – the cost of heating them may take another dive in personal gain.

To gain, you might draw the card that says "Pass go, and drive directly to the gas station that has lowered its daily price per gallon." But the card may also say, "Go directly to jail and file bankruptcy because you can't afford to heat your properties."

That's okay; the jail is heated.

There is a free parking space, but it takes a full tank to get there and the only gas station along the way has just raised its prices 20 cents per gallon since yesterday when it suddenly reduced the price for the hag's car with a full tank.

Landing on "Waterworks" and the "Electric Company" can be iffy because the owners may be sneaky and look for ways to raise rates by claiming a water shortage due to tsunamis in Iowa and electrical storms that occur while kite-flying. They want a piece of the pie, after all.

There is hope, however, around the Gaspoloy board. It is possible, for instance, to land on the sought-after square called "Collect a windfall lottery."

Just as you get diamonds in your eyes and think you're going to beat the game, you read the fine print which says, "But pay the accountant, IRS and forgotten loans from your mother-in-law. Not to mention the 50-cent loan you took at work to buy a candy bar from the vending machine."

Put Gasopoly on your things-to-play list because it can teach younger, future drivers that life is just another game.

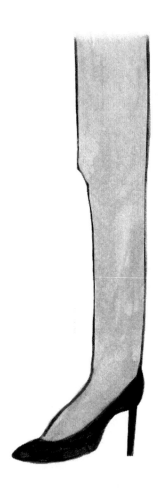

# THe CaNKLeS Report

I t's a new definition of non-shaped calf muscles that point two parallel lines straight down through the ankles, the combined effect being, "cankles." No shapely legs, just two swizzle sticks. It's just yet another physical flaw that women must endure while flipping through fashion magazines featuring perfect sized two bodies.

Cankles used to be called, "piano legs," most unflattering beneath skirt hems. No matter how sleek and trendy the rest of your outfit, piano legs ruin it. Two very large men just might show up and roll you across the floor with squeaky wheels and position you next to the bar. There you would just be big and dumb, smiling through piano teeth.

The body flaws list has a long history for women. For men, my ex-husband simply summed up their male flaws with, "My body is a cage for my head." But with women, there's a whole repertoire of reasons to flunk the appearance glitches. Most common are love handles, or landles, the kind that make door knobs look sophisticated. If you can pinch an inch, then it's time for the elastic report. I once thought that I could actually pinch a foot, but was mistaken when I accidentally included several other falling body attachments. The solution to that is not about the hemline, but a large sized surgical shroud in the middle.

The widow's hump, or wump, is another curiosity about aging women. I don't know the original meaning behind the widow part. Probably that a poor, pathetic woman was without her man, so she had to cast her eyes downward in despair. With men, it's more sophisticated as in, "surgeon's neck," or something to appear professional and important. In women, it's an unsightly hump to again flunk the fashion magazines. I'll probably develop one trying to read the aspirin bottle.

And thus, the fashion advice for victims of cankles has to do with the position of the hem. If just below the knee, then that would emphasize how dopey you look and soon the piano movers would show up. If at the ankle, then all would be forgiven and you would be allowed to carry on intelligent conversations without causing a public spectacle.

Then, of course, there are specific anti-cankle exercises that transform you from a grand piano to a shapely runway model in one day. They are, as you might expect, sweating through some rises upward onto the tippy toes, doing some aerobic jumps while wearing high heels and a few cartwheels thrown in.

I used to do all these things with ease, of course, when my youth was being wasted on my youth. But these days if I rise up on my tippy toes, the right leg jumps around into a tremor of spasms jutting up and down preparing for a major quake. Then the calf muscle retreats into a solid golf ball-shaped Charley Horse leaving my heel stuck several inches from the floor and agony stuck on my face. The solution is to stretch all this out and hope that my legs soon match each other with the same dimensions. The facial agony will probably remain, just like when I was a child and warned that if I crossed my eyes, they might get stuck.

There are also shoe fashions to camouflage the suffering cankle-challenged. Most have additional parade float material to give shape to the bottom of the leg. The trouble is, the calves look even more cankled. A dire situation. Well, maybe a little surgical enhancement up there will do, if not some cankle-friendly hems that add bulk.

My solution to cankles and all flaws yet to be defined is a very large tent.

# Recovering From
## 'Post Traumatic Checkbook Syndrome'

**M**any are experiencing the symptoms, but fail to realize it at the time. Until it's too late. Then a proper meltdown of lucid thinking requires hyperventilating in the beginning and intense therapy in the end.

I noticed some red flags of PTCS hovering the other day when I opened my checkbook and moths flew out. I swear that one of them flew around my head and chirped, "Oh, oh, trouble lurks ahead." Then, when I wrote the check to the grocery store checker, my hand began shaking uncontrollably. She was suspicious and ran a complete criminal background check.

"OK, lighten up," I told her, "so I'll remove the citronella in the designer jar, the flowers on sale and the anti-aging vitamins," I begged her, "but please leave the fresh strawberries and the check should be good."

That was the first sign that the checkbook was ailing. Then when my debit card ran through the gas pump slot, the screen blinked, "you are broke, you are broke." I threw myself into the windshield wash and attempted hagacide right there at Pump #4 until the service station person convinced me that the screen really meant, "you are ugly, you are ugly."

Relieved that I was only ugly and not broke -- at least at this fill up – I exhibited cocky spending behavior and bought designer water from the other side of the planet.

Then, there have been times when my checkbook has dry heaves, a sure sign that there's nothing in its stomach. I have come to its rescue, however, and treated it with a rubber massage, a temporary fix designed not to bounce back by a certain date.

But recently my checkbook threatened to belly up on the desk. The little pad was choking and the cover was in shreds. It lay there pathetic and ashen. At the same time, a suspicious bank envelope appeared in the mailbox. It was then that I had to administer life support in an emergency situation.

I have always tried to avoid Check Book Rigor Mortis because the fees are simply too great for an oversight. But when your finances are fairly close – like hand to big mouth – an occasional checkbook intravenous is in order.

I once ran over to the bank and threw myself across an officer's desk with a choking check book in hand. "Where did I fail?" was my plea and hoped that we could unravel the checkbook's intestines to clear up a mistake.

"Well," she snickered, "it seems that you remembered to notate your drive-through high fat quarter pound cheeseburger with fries, onion rings and a cookie." She glanced at my stomach. "But you forgot about the Chinese takeout without MSG the next day for $8.65 plus tax."

She obviously had no sense of humor when I claimed that at least my diet was improving even if my checkbook was failing. "Hmmph," was her response as she held me at ransom for the checkbook recovery program.

I asked her if my government stimulus check was there, thinking that I had the edge. Money is power, you know. She told me that it was the fastest deposit and withdrawal transaction in the bank's history. The thing came and went in the same digit hour leaving feathers in its database. My checkbook never even noticed that I didn't buy a broad side of a barn-sized screen TV or a calcu/camera/coffee-making cell phone equipped to download music from Siberia.

My poor checkbook still lies there recovering from PTCS, a dread disease for which there is no recovery in sight.

# Practicing Sleepus Interruptus

I t's a regular dysfunction that we all occasionally suffer from. Sleepus Interruptus has become a popular malady in this frenetic and fast-paced world to put sleep at the bottom of the priority list. That way, we can prove that we are hard-working pillars of the community and professional keepers of the Earth. Enough sleep? No, I was practicing to be the next Mother Teresa or campaigning to be the next president.

Lack of sleep is also a good way to be ugly, crabby and have episodes of emotional breakdowns over minor inconveniences. I came from the store without toilet paper one day, then couldn't find my glasses in the same day. I fell helplessly onto the couch and proved an air-tight case that my whole life was a failure. Nothing eight hours of sleep couldn't remedy.

But somehow we as a society value the idea that getting regular sleep is for the weak and lowly. Physicians, airline pilots and other injun' chiefs that play with our lives everyday must constantly prove that they don't need enough sleep. Not to mention the other journalists, shift workers and shopkeepers who brag to their captives about the "24-7" schedule when life is one big nervous whirligig.

You can't blame us totally for our sleepless society. Mother Nature started it first. Initially, She gave us peace and quiet in darkened bedrooms without alarm clocks. We would arise rested and stretch to embrace the day. I've seen this idea portrayed in mattress commercials or travelogues that depict the ultimate in relaxation with ocean breezes gently wafting over dreamy afternoon naps.

Some of us in our youth continued to sleep soundly at the wrong times. Miss Haswell's Latin I class was occasionally interrupted by a snore or two. I always slept through alarm clocks quite well, but finally stirred

163

at my mother's piercing shouts at the bottom of the stairs.

But then Mother Nature invented newborns, or the first act of Sleepus Interruptus. Every two hours around the clock they have to be fed and have diapers changed in between while fathers never seem to hear crying in the next room. (Oh, that's right, I'm supposed to remember that he changed a diaper once, somewhere in the '70s.)

Then Mother Nature decided it befitting to have mothers with dark circles and haggard glares, so She invented two-year-olds that specialize in search-and-destroy techniques that never wear out.

In order to assure safety to our little ones, we sacrificed years of sleep to maintain a constant heightened state of alertness. The children at your side one minute can be missing the next. I was paged at a department store once, "Will the mother of little girl with blue dress and green shoes please come to the cookie department?" Or at the bank, she once told a teller that, "her mom was lost," not her. My two-year-old son let himself out of the house one Sunday morning, shed his shorts somewhere in the alley and headed for the sandbox two blocks away. I didn't sleep for the next ten years.

The Sleepus Interruptus era in Mother Nature's next cruel joke is the invention of teenagers. If they are in the house, the decibels are always at an unacceptable level at unacceptable times. If the house is eerily quiet, it means that teenagers are out perhaps getting in trouble. No sleep again.

Sleepus Interruptus will likely be the ultimate population control. With everyone's dark circles, crabby dispositions and ugly expressions, males and females will give each other the creeps and thus stay away from each other.

# Putting a Lid On It

With all the global wars out there, the biggest controversy has always been whether toilet lids should be up or down. The battle lines are clearly drawn and, as you might expect, the male guard says up and the female front line says down.

I even had a male acquaintance who took his toilet lid politics so far as to completely write off an actress who chose not to live with the opposing force that armed themselves with lids up. If she fiercely defended her house to be lidded-down, then he would therefore boycott her movies. It made complete sense to him.

Having lived apart from the enemy camp of lids up for many years, I haven't been too involved in this heated debate. I always noticed that my ex-husband's house, populated by a mostly male faction, has a strategic war plan to have the lids up. Part of the strategy is to eliminate ex-wives whose noses wrinkled upward upon entering his bathroom. It was also convenient for his canine member of the force to have fresh, porcelain-chilled water handy to slurp at all hours.

We females on this side of the battleground, have our lids properly down, freshly scented with pink soap nearby. If during a male invasion on a holiday or so, someone left the lid up, I would completely sterilize the toilet, wall behind it, floor beneath it and feel thankful that my personal space was normally untainted by the toilet lid enemy. So the lid foe receded forces and I was left without much hostility because, after all, the enemy was gone.

Then I nearly fell through the city sewer system recently. I sank into the abyss of creepiness with my legs pointing toward the ceiling. My kneecaps were before my eyes and sweet-smelling pajamas were suddenly diseased. My thighs gave out too soon and I sank with a "Whoa!" It was too late to climb upward, so I came afloat with an extreme case of the creeps. I was convinced that every killer disease in the world was after me by the time I got myself upright again. My rear end was tainted, and it was nothing like the outhouses of my youth. Those were the ones with a moon overhead and breezes on your rear end. No thank you.

So when I recovered my rear end from all things terrible, I saw my six-year-old grandson sleeping sweetly around the corner. He was dreaming about toilet lids and I had a diseased rear end. He was the culprit, and I knew that he had been brainwashed by the enemy, the enemy that leaves lids up. He suddenly was not looking so angelic as he slept, I noticed.

I'm not sure what the answer is, but the enemy had clearly been indoctrinated to invade my house with a lid left up. And I didn't know where my next strategy would lead me next in the War of Lids.

I understand that there are some fancy, high end toilet designs available at high cost to disarm the sexes with an automatic feature that returns to the down position after use by a male. I think. Or does the entire bathroom return to sterilized, fresh-scented with pink soap nearby after the male leaves? I forget, but it's too expensive for most of our humble households to have automatic lids up or down services.

Now. Here's my question that has nothing to do with the direction of this column, but nevertheless important: Have any of you males (the enemy) ever unwittingly sat down on a toilet in the darkness with the lid up? Just curious...

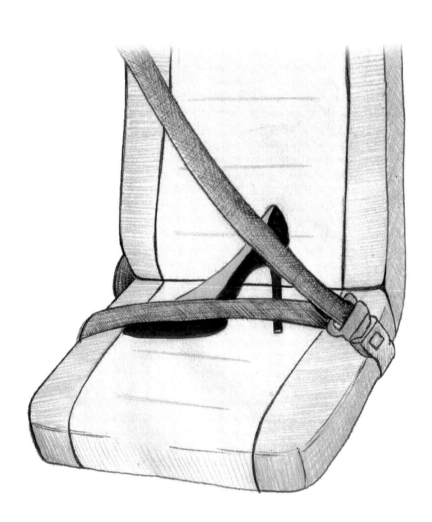

# Flunking Car Seat 101

Sure, I went to school and somehow along the way got a four-year degree. Like most college students pursuing an academic goal, I had to survive various lab sciences, English courses, history surveys and even a quick test on our state government.

What universities ought to require in their curriculum these days is Car Seat 101. That would really weed out the lightweights. Especially unsuspecting new grandmothers that have already raised children in 1972 Mustangs or used Chevy something-or-others without seat belts.

My newborn son, in fact, was hand-delivered to me in the passenger seat by a hospital nurse standing in the mud and rain. I had already argued with my husband about parking illegally and holding up traffic. We practically sped off before I could even shut the car door, newborn in tow.

Then when we drove from Chicago to Florida on some vacation, the baby slept on my lap. The only road hazards were my husband's tailgating and my permanently damp lap due to his refusal to stop the car long enough to change a diaper.

Then my daughter had some sort of car seat, but no directions as thick as a standard Anthology of American Literature to operate the thing. Two simple straps came around, the baby was in and I drove off. The only hazard was that in Chicago traffic I kept turning around to admire my perfect little girl in her pink ruffles.

So here comes the next generation, and a whole new world of car seats. My daughter studied the directions in the living room before her baby was born. She opened up the folding map and instantly made sense of the arrows, clicks and safety suggestions. She got it, I didn't. It was headlined "some assembly required" (bad start) and the need for a course in Car Seat 101.

169

Two belts came down and across the chest, right over left (or was it left over right?), attached to another belt that came from underneath to spiral around a baby-techno-gizmo and clicked into another torso fairy button that sings lullabies while blowing kisses. At the first whimper, there is yet another button to strap in everyone bumping heads in the back seat to cool tempers.

This is after the other set of belts that attach to the car. For that, there's another anthology chapter for rear-facing versus front-facing babies complete with a weight and height chart of all participating family members including grandmothers whose stomachs hang out.

After the baby was born, it was soon discovered that a second car seat was in order. In two car families, or in this case on the farm, old car and one-ton truck, it was too much trouble for one seat to go back and forth.

The second seat turned out to be a bit more grandmother-friendly for those who haven't taken Car Seat 101. So I happily used that one in my car until my son-in-law unwittingly absconded with it and jerry-rigged it to the field combine. When I protested, he said that it was now permanently attached to the combine unless, of course, he needed it in the one-ton truck.

I appealed to my daughter and said that I honestly couldn't understand how to attach the anthology-instructed car seat. What was I to do about taking my most perfect grandson somewhere if I couldn't operate the car seat?

"OK mom, concentrate," she felt sorry for me. And she went through the right over left stuff while we bumped heads to examine the gizmo belt inserted into the fairy button. My eyes glazed over.

But I failed again while her eyes rolled upward because I flunked Car Seat 101.

# Shot in the Heart By Saint Valentine

Somehow, we got from a charming third century legend to a commercial industry that amounts to some kind of a sham. The hearts are just too big, the chocolates too heart-shaped and the message too large.

Don't get me wrong, I think that a romantic day to spread happiness and good will once a year is a delightful idea.

But what I notice about the historic martyr St. Valentine is that he brought flowers from his garden to the women. Then they threw him flowers when he was imprisoned.

There must be something missing from the story because he was the last male on earth since 269 A.D. to initiate the idea of flowers all by himself. That means, "Oh!" (and a light bulb appears over a male's head) "I think I'll bring my lady some flowers or a heart-shaped something."

I'm convinced, anyway, by my own Valentine's Day history.

I think it all started when I never got a Valentine card from the cute boy in the fifth grade. I was crushed. I looked all around me to see that the other giggling, tee-heeing girls got cutouts that said "BEE my Valentine" from a smiling bumblebee. I just got the standard heart-shaped candy from the teacher who didn't like me, anyway, because I once cheated on a spelling test.

But did those giggling girls really get the bumblebee cutouts from the cute boy? I am suspicious these days that the mother was behind it. I simply cannot imagine that a fifth-grader with a gleam in his eye reported to the dime store for just the right bumblebee cutout.

Then as I became a teenager, I watched my cheerleading friends "go steady" right and left with the cute guys. They exchanged bulky class rings that she layered with thread and fingernail polish to make it fit. I still don't remember those cute steadies worrying about hearts and flowers. He was busy hunching his shoulders just right with his collar up to appear cool.

Since then, the cute boy concept has eluded me. I have heard of falling in love at first sight with heartthrobs while prancing about – he shows up with flowers behind his back. Or, seeing someone across the crowded room who happens to have a small velvet box in hand.

Most of my male relationships, however, sort of fell in the back door with all the romantic notions of a tree stump, grinning and bearing a thoughtful can of WD40.

I married one of them. It wasn't a gripping proposal from the knees like a live talk show event, but rather when the car stalled in an alley and he found that opportunity to say, "ah, er, (hunched shoulders) do you think that we should get married, then?" It followed an unrelated subject about my changing jobs.

There were no romantic diamonds or engagement rocks, just gold bands. That was fine, except then I lost mine down the furnace vent. By the time I got my next band, the marriage went down the furnace vent, also. My husband never observed calendars, either. He once accused them of harassment. He wanted his daily routines served without the inconvenience of worrying about hearts and flowers some day in February.

I had another male friend who actually brought me flowers all by himself. They were day-old and a bit wilted from the compost heap at his flower nursery job, but hey, it was the thought that counted. He still hunched his shoulders while presenting them so not for a moment to let down his masculine guard.

It's not that males are completely oblivious about romance. They just need a little prodding sometimes because there seems no program pre-loaded in their testosterone to hear orchestras or heartthrobs all by themselves.

Maybe that's why the hearts and flowers are so big in the store. HINT, HINT! It's Valentine's Day, you idiot!

# Sleeping For Another Hundred Years

I glanced out the kitchen window the other day and realized that my back yard suddenly looked like the overgrown forest in "Sleeping Beauty."

I was instantly overwhelmed because it seemed that I had it all coifed and clipped the day before. I must have overslept about a hundred years. Either that or maybe my lawnmower needs a little work, like a direct trip to the landfill.

I have had this illustrious hand push mower for several decades. Even then it was already a bit of garage history from another long lost friend. I resurrected it, had it sharpened and hooked up the grass catcher thinking that I would single-handedly save the planet. If I liked the whole process, then I planned to paint it purple to match the wise Lilac Fairy in "Sleeping Beauty."

Well, the reel part turns, though the roller part is a bit askew. The main problem is that it doesn't cut grass. The blades lie down and instantly pop back up before I even sneeze. The dandelions snicker and the crabgrass claps its leaves.

It turns out that all I have done is save myself the trouble of dying from ordinary diseases and instead dying from mowing over the same spot 18 times. It's what happens when hags get lofty ideas about sleeping princesses on green planets to be awakened by handsome princes who happen to know how to sharpen lawnmowers.

So if I'm not allowed to sleep another hundred years, I'm going to have to face the music about the lawnmower dilemma. My real problem is that I just don't like grass to begin with. It just sits there. If I wanted something to be boring and green, I'd hire a set designer with a paintbrush. No dastardly machinery necessary. I just want to mosey around in pointe shoes, sniff my blooms, cut some for vase arrangements and listen to the opera.

But back to reality with no handsome princes in sight, I have to have something to cut the little grass I have. The way I see it, there are several options. I could just leave it at the curb for an enterprising prince to come along. But my luck would be that even a gathering of magic junk collectors would bypass this diamond in the rough.

There is also the option to just throw in the towel and report to the credit card fairies for a new lawnmower. But having had a rather mouthy argument with a credit card fairy recently about the sneaky, incorrect late fee, I wasn't in the mood to whip out the card and tempt fate. The wolf might show up at the door wearing a ballet tutu.

Another option is to forget green planets and resort to the aging power mower that I already have. My main concern about that is the noise factor. I just want to cut the grass and not awaken the entire neighborhood whose sleep schedule is not in the same fairytale as mine.

So I reported to the gas station, risking headlines about exploding hags, and returned with the evil fairy's gas can in hand to fill it up. By the time I turned my back to admire my flowers, the gas had promptly leaked out the bottom and down the driveway. It looks like that mower will go to the magic curb fairies, also.

Another option is to just go back to sleep for another hundred years and dream that a more mechanically inclined prince shows up. I don't care what he looks like next time.

# THe CoNSpiratoriaL LaWNMoWer

I t sat in the garage all winter, looking innocent enough. I now know better.

For six months, I came and went, shoveled and salted and warmed up the car. I barely noticed it sitting next to the barbecue and tomato stakes. It blended into the trappings of another season, another life.

What my lawnmower really did was twiddle its blades and plan my demise.

"Wait until spring," it whispered to the coiled garden hose. The timing should be perfect, it thought, and best in April when the grass is suddenly thick and clumpy – preferably when the rest of the block is already freshly mowed looking like landscapes in "Better Homes and Gardens" magazine.

Then, with its first moment in the sun, it would roar right into this season's attack. Somewhere between its piston and pull cord is the stored memory of a malicious felon. It remembers with total recall the offenses that remind me that its primary goal in life is to ruin a perfectly sunny day. With the social conscience of a hag killer, I know that my lawnmower is out to get me.

The first offense is when it lies there faint and empty-tanked. Its red cover is pale and wan. That's a setup that forces me to risk life and limb with the gas can. The possible headline would be, "Hag explodes near gas station."

Then comes the driveway drama that might be better known as the "starting stalemate." The lawnmower finds it amusing while I must recover with aspirin. I circle pensively deciding just how much to prime. Some lawnmowers need more stabs to wake up its innards.

But if I prime too much, it develops a gorge-purge disorder and pretends to be legally dead.

Then comes the tug-of-war phase that includes shouts, four-letter words and slamming doors. There are phone calls to any answering machine available to announce how a perfectly sunny day has been ruined.

Once my blood pressure is up, face red and shoulder dislocated, the mower puts out one pathetic cough. It is still just pretending. The neighbors peer through parted curtains to see what the commotion is about.

Meantime, I develop a theory about why no one else seems to own a conspiratorial lawnmower. I notice that mowers have a pull cord designed for right-handers. In order to get the correct leverage to pull, us left-handers must stand a giant scissors-step to the right and prop a foot against the neighbor's fence.

By then, my mower is really on the aggressive attack against my sanity. It remembers some things and forgets others. Like last year when I hoisted its ungainly parts, rear bag and all in a car trunk the size of my purse. With clumsy tentacles sideswiping street signs, it threatened to leap out while I inched toward the sharpening shop.

It has forgotten that the lawnmower guy cleaned, conditioned and sharpened. It had a halo over its engine when I picked it up, all smiles and ready to go.

But the moment it was home and running, it regurgitated a steady stream of grass clippings that pointed directly at me. I was the one on the block with a whirling private green tornado as I mowed. It had sprung a spring, and scored again.

The most serious affliction that my lawnmower has suffered is when I once used it to help a neighbor. I was a good Samaritan, but my mower didn't like the foreign territory with a cast iron water plug sticking out of the ground.

It's been against me ever since.

# SPring CLeaNiNg tHe FaMiLy GeNes

**F**amily studies show that dysfunctional behaviors tend to travel within the family. Alcoholism, for instance, often repeats its cycle in following generations as do other various abuses.

Within my family is a serious dysfunction called, "Obsessive Housekeeping Syndrome," or OHS. Though the disease is not officially listed among mental illnesses except perhaps the compulsive-obsessive area, it nevertheless leaves crippling scars that last a lifetime.

The earliest symptoms of the disease were part of my childhood memories. I had an aunt who shouted military orders by the hour to anyone standing still about what to clean next. No self-respecting dust-mite could have settled for a moment in that household. She set the record straight about having bookshelves around. "They collect too much dust," she complained.

Luckily, she already knew everything so there was no need for those germ-infested books around the house, anyway.

The most deranged form of OHS appeared in my parents. My step-dad couldn't exercise enough control over the world. He couldn't control those unkempt beards or long hair in the '60s. He couldn't control those messy art forms that cluttered his reality with nonsense. He couldn't control that rebellious and disorderly generation that planted flowers and talked about "organic gardening."

Most seriously, however, was the fact that he couldn't control that unhygienic habit of people touching each other with affectionate ardor. All those "sloppy kisses and hugs" were acts of undisciplined behavior, he thought. Sexual activity anywhere in the world without his permission was right up there with murder.

In order to rid himself of life's messy images, he commanded a perfect house with my mother's doormat devotion. Every room, basement area and closet was scrubbed and orderly at all times. The walls had no paintings – art was clutter – dinner dishes were swept away before the last bite and beds were made before you were up. Each blade of grass outside stood and saluted in perfect unison without the interference of disorderly flowers or vegetables that those long hairs used nasty compost on.

My mother, of course, never questioned anything, so she has been cleaning now for more than 50 years straight.

Then there was my husband the Nervous-Nelly cleaner. While his goal of a clean house is admirable, his real OHS affliction is the need to be in motion at all times. Some people gesture a lot, smoke or chew their nails. He cleans.

If you talk to him about something face to face like, "one of the children is missing," he suddenly dives downward to get that spot at the bottom of the refrigerator.

His fascination with annoying noises also finds itself in OHS. As a youngster he probably did the normal male progression from disgusting armpit noises to car engine revs. By far, however, his favorite noise as an adult is the vacuum cleaner. He roars through peace and quiet for hours, never pausing a moment to blow his nose. The dog went to a different floor. The children escaped outside. I moved to a different city.

Thankfully, I am happy to announce that I have successfully stopped the crippling cycle of OHS. I can actually sit down and read a book with full knowledge that there might be a cat hair in the front hallway and a spider web in the basement.

# Getting the Skinny On Fat

**M**irror, mirror...

By now we should be finished with all those lofty New Year's resolutions. Especially the one about losing weight and becoming an Olympic contender to look like a Greek statue of a muscular showcase for excellence.

The diets have turned sour, the exercise equipment takes up too much room and frequently needs dusting. And public places seem to me the last place to wear something revealing like a swimsuit, though my friends tell me that I would be horrified at the hanging objects and cascading wrinkles found at the local pool.

I might suggest that those blabber-mouthed mirrors are major enemies from the very beginning of our lives. When I was young, the mirror, mirror on the wall said that I should look like Doris Day singing, "Que Sera Sera," in her latest coloring book. A little later, that loudmouth mirror said that I should be like those skinny models in "Seventeen" magazine wearing the latest fall fashions for school.

Having those studio mirrors in ballet class around was like having your own personal sniping Greek chorus glaring and abusing you for the hour and a half that you are there. They sing in a minor key, "if you were thinner, you could do that step," and, "you cannot possibly believe that you'll ever dance looking like that!" And then, of course, you become obsessed with what those abusive mirrors say about you from day to day until you develop a minor diet disorder.

Before you walk down the aisle, some ominous mirror warns you that this is the last day you'll be thin enough for a wedding dress. It also says that when you partake of that piece of wedding cake, your first waist roll will suddenly appear. After that, says that mirror who won't mind its own business, the marriage won't be one made in heaven.

Then after giving birth, there's always a wet blanket mirror that tells you how ugly you are, have way too much baby fat and no child will grow to love that. Thirty years later, I'm convinced by some mirror around the house that I still have baby fat.

And the mirrors everywhere keep nagging that you should look like skinny models and anorexic actresses who live on portions of food that require binoculars to see on the plate.

I passed a restaurant mirror the other night and it told me that I was much fatter than I remembered at home 15 minutes before. It must be lying, I thought, but it got belligerent and pointed fingers at my stomach that had not yet digested the evening special. Just for that, I told that ugly mirror, I'm not going to look.

Since I think that most mirrors are like those misshapen fat images at the circus, anyway, I might suggest that not looking at mirrors is the first key to mental health. Then you can just go around and think of yourself as 30 pounds thinner. There's no one to argue with, be abused by or get depressed over.

That was my real New Year's resolution; not to look. Then I can eat my chocolate in peace and quiet without judgment from those no good, useless and unemployed mirrors that don't know what they're talking about, anyway.

A friend pointed out the other day, however, that my makeup was a bit sideways and my hair was shaped like a trapezoid. There was also toothpaste on my chin. I informed her that I wasn't speaking to mirrors anymore, so that's how I would probably look.

The trouble is, now the walls are talking. It's not my imagination, either, because I overheard some whispers from the closet when I got out a skirt to wear.

# Successful Failures in 2011

For most of us enterprising New Year revelers, the resolutions have gone by the wayside.

We've settled into our old ways, whether fat, frumpy or addicted. That's one thing I learned while in my ballet addiction of younger days. The body is most stubborn about maintaining habits, good or bad. If the body is used to donuts and couches, then it wants to have those donuts and couches with the path of least resistance. And likewise, if the body is addicted to healthy habits and exercise, it wants to maintain that, also.

But when it comes to changing those habits, the body is enormously stubborn, inefficient and has a poor memory. Basically, whoever we were in December of last year is who we are now.

It was then, for instance, that twice I approached my refrigerator and stole designer chocolate with the darkest ingredient – it's healthy, after all – that had been designated as a gift for someone else. It is therefore extremely unlikely that this month I will be able to have designer chocolate with the darkest ingredient around the house. I simply lose control when it comes to chocolate.

And, of course, the predictable New Year's resolution experts have come out of the media-work raising a forefinger about how we should proceed with our virtuous life improvements. They warn us not to set our goals higher than we can accomplish so that we don't set ourselves up for failure.

That's advice worth heeding. One year, I resolved to become an Olympic runner by April. With clenched fist, eyes narrowed and doing jumping jacks, I toasted champagne at midnight to the new and improved me.

185

But, I conveniently forgot about two previous knee surgeries, arthritis and a sciatic attack that left a numb foot. So much for the Olympics.

Another year, I resolved to be the poster hag for carrot juice. Still determined to overhaul my health, I did jumping jacks at midnight and planned to cleanse my system of toxic foods and focus entirely on a monk's diet of vegetable juices, vitamins and energy drinks. By February, I envisioned, I would feel so good that I couldn't resist running marathons. Ah, my body is my temple, I thought, like the health gurus proclaim.

But then I conveniently forgot about that addictive chocolate and necessary caffeine to jittery jump-start each day. To my knowledge, there is no local coffee rehab center in the area.

So if diet and exercise fail, maybe I should change myself. Maybe I should make better use of time, balance the check book more often or not procrastinate so much. Maybe, I even thought, I should resolve to keep my brain more active and learn another language or read music each day.

But, again, by mid January, the virtuous and responsible life was simply too dull. The language center of my brain has long since turned into a petrified forest and the piano is embarrassingly out of tune.

Another self-improvement attempt was during a "kinder, gentler" era when I could be a little more like Mother Teresa and less like the Wicked Witch of the West. But again, my chiseled glare at my ex-husband leaked through the wrinkles. Besides, a nun's habit on me might scare small children.

I even researched Pollyanna. But it occurred to me right away that this chickie never made a living, endured teenagers, paid a tax bill or did laundry. No wonder that she is listed in the dictionary as "foolishly optimistic."

So much for Pollyanna and the rest of New Year's resolutions. I have therefore resolved to buy more expensive wine, eat more chocolate, buy designer coffee beans, procrastinate more and make all the ugly faces I want. Guaranteed success, the resolution experts would agree.

I feel better already.

# Paint the Town Pink!

Some of us are a little slow to realize what is going on. It all began with Breast Cancer Awareness month. I couldn't help but notice the pink ribbon in print all around as if nagging me to do something responsible.

Mind you, I don't often tune into this or that month when we're supposed to suddenly care about something and forget about it the rest of the year. When it comes to health, in fact, I always said that they'll have to come get me for the diagnosis. I don't relish sitting around waiting rooms waiting to wait.

But I woke up recently and looked in the mirror. It was the usual horror story looking back at me with wrinkles, falling body parts and excess adipose tissue – you know, 35 years ago equals 35 extra pounds at the rate of just one teensy-weensy pound per year.

Never mind the math, however, because what I saw in this horrifying mirror moment was a huge bruise. The next day, there seemed to be some white lump in the middle. By the time my old hag friends gathered to gossip on Saturday evening, I questioned all of our knowledge about breast cancer. And there were horror stories about this or that friend who died and whomever didn't obey the medical rules of the most recent test to determine every hangnail.

I countered that my grandmother lived until 96 with no vice grip clamping down on her body parts nor some country doctor with a nurse on hand to invade her privacy. My friends tell me that those times have changed.

So we agreed that it was time for me to report to the mammogram police and check in with the peek-a-boo doctors. All turned out fine, but the episode took on real meaning when I looked around to see that all is not necessarily fine with other women.

And, of course, the same week that I had to report to the Boring Medical Authorities, I had to get the car oil changed and have routine teeth cleaning. Please don't put me to sleep with all this regular life stuff.

Then I couldn't help but notice that Breast Cancer Awareness month had this strong pink theme. Hey, I like pastel colors and pink is perfectly appropriate for some things. After all, men don't generally wear it. We women, though, knit pink items for our children and grandchildren. We also enjoy pink here and there in everything else. There are pink boots, pink jackets, pink everything. And pink watches! After all, girls are made of sugar and spice, everything nice, and probably pink. Why not?

And there's a strong pink bandwagon out there because we women are strong! We can lick this disease if we just be more responsible about reporting to the mammogram police frequently.

So with the latest knowledge that I survived Breast Cancer Awareness month and that I would probably live at least until this edition, I painted my back door shocking pink. While the paint can was open, I painted my mailbox pink. The garage door might be next. And before I'm done, the front door is suspect.

If you still procrastinate responsible things in life like I do, get that quick, easy mammogram, and paint the town pink afterwards!

# THat DreadFul "C" Word

There are so many males that seem to have an inordinate fear of the "C" word. No, not the scary "commitment" word that housekeeping magazines do feature articles about. It's a simple word that rattles the entire gender right down to the boxer shorts.

*Change.*

I base my sweeping generalization on scientific research gathered from over 30 years of behavioral studies. The resulting, "Ridiculous file," so far unchallenged, follows the observations of just one male subject – Kong-rad the ex-husband.

According to this study, whenever the word "change" is uttered in any conversation, the male subject begins twitching and shivering from head to toe. Stuttering follows as he grapples nervously for intelligent reasons why the frightful "change" is impossible. There is usually an increase of sweating at this stage.

Virtually any kind of change nearly causes a medical emergency. Change of clothes, change of location, change of the sock drawer.

I have heard women bashers in other studies laugh that some males drag their knuckles on the ground. In this particular Kong-rad study, the drag is at the other end – most noticeably his heels.

I should have noticed this early in the marriage when I decided to change the bedroom furniture around. He spent the next six months irritable because he couldn't find his underwear. Apparently, he had already memorized the exact bedroom map for life and couldn't adjust to such a change.

The next bad sign is when he wanted my first pregnancy to last for the rest of my life. "Why change?" he exclaimed. "All the baby's needs are being taken care of now."

191

Then along came some research that indicated diet changes for healthier living. A further assault was yogurt on the market and in our refrigerator.

He grew up in his mother's kitchen where red meat was incinerated, vegetables were incarcerated, and potatoes were white. Yogurt and fresh vegetables? That would be a fearful change.

And, speaking of food, where was his young wife at that exact hour everyday when he scratched himself and grunted, "huh, duh, what's for dinner?" At ballet class or rehearsal, where else?

After that, I learned never to discuss change again. I simply did it. If I wanted a dog, I brought it home. If I wanted different wallpaper, I hung it. If I wanted a child, I planned it.

I also noticed that he couldn't seem to process several activities at once. His aversion to even minor changes seemed to affect his physical coordination. For instance, I could nurse a baby, talk on the phone, stir something on the stove, tell the dog to lie down AND think about something else at the same time.

He was able to walk straight ahead, pause, then pick up a tool, provided no one asked him a question at the same time. "Could you take out the trash?" No. That's overload. He was busy walking a straight line.

He once stormed home with such agony that I thought that there had been a major tragedy. He pace and stewed, then finally shouted that the hardware store had changed its aisles around. The tools were in the wrong place!

Based on this important Kong-rad study about an aversion to change, I did some historical research to find if caveman had the same affliction. While inventing the wheel, for instance, I wondered if the caveman stared straight ahead with his single-minded blinders in place. He likely scratched his head, stewed and said "hmmm" for a few centuries. Then once accomplished, he probably belched with his buddies for a few more centuries.

But meantime, cavewoman probably had better ideas for his change. In the cave while nursing, stirring something and telling the wolf to lie down, she likely spent only five minutes transforming the wheel into a shopping cart. Caveman was still saying "Hurumph."

In fact, man is probably responsible for the Dark Ages. No change, no change.

# It's the Bees Knees

I said something about "the bees knees" to a friend the other day and she wagged a forefinger that I was showing my age.

The truth is, I never heard this expression when I was younger. There may have been a bar called, "The purple cow," or a shop called, "The Polka Dots," but never have I heard of a stinging insect that buzzes about having knees.

I have been stung by one here and there when I have unwittingly invaded the territory of an enterprising bee. But amid the hysteria, I forgot to look closer and discover if there were knee caps or, for that matter, thighs or calves. I am not going to run out to the garden right now, either, because it would be my luck to find a glaring bee showing its teeth at me. I am not even sure, at this writing, if bees have teeth, but I am not taking any chances.

Furthermore, there seems no definition in any reference books. That's when it is time to define it for myself. When in doubt, I always say, make it up. It is much more adventurous.

"The bees knees," I understand, is supposed to be a positive description, like, "the berries." I get the one about berries, because they are special fruits with a pleasant taste. But a bee with knees is a horse of a different color. In my mind, if a bee really has knees, he would think twice about how great life is. For one thing, knees deteriorate with time and lots of kneeling. Wings seem everlasting, but look out for bending over a flower everyday.

Thus, the act of constantly pollinating in a bent position will eventually cause arthritis and swelling making it necessary to have knee replacement by the time it reports back to the hive.

The queen bee will be miffed and react with hostility at the idea that a crippled worker convalesces too long away from the job. Furthermore, there is no guarantee that kneeling will be fully restored in the future. Then the cost of bees knees rehab!

So the bees knees have suddenly turned into a bumbled situation where a regular wage worker bee needs to make an honest living and keep buzzing with honey income and benefits.

Aside from the medical issues about having knees, there is the attractiveness idea. If a worker bee doesn't thrill the queen with greased thighs and calves while flexing his muscles, then there may be some favoritism elsewhere, like in the Mr. Buzz World Contest. The body-building bees sweat away at lifting heavy coneflowers and beefsteak tomatoes until their muscles shine.

But inevitably, the abuses of injecting illicit tree sap will cause buzz-failure for the most extreme imbibers. Flexing no more, the bee returns to a lowlife of pollinating low class dandelions only.

If the worker bees have knees, then the queen must have knees also. If she resides in a shoe (oh whoops, wrong fairytale), or rather a hive, then she must look attractive at all times for her string of muscle-flexing suitors. One problem, however, is that she is not able to wear Stiletto heels around the honeycomb. If she can't buzz upright in heels, then her calves and thighs don't look right.

The queen's real problem about having knees, however, is that she is worn down trying to run a big operation. Her bottom line says to make honey faster and faster with these lowlife workers that can't even kneel properly to her orders.

Having bees knees is not exactly the bees knees, after all.

# Hats OFF to Hats OFF

While spring is springing, there is usually renewed focus on fashion hats. Flowers, petals, maybe a bird nest or two in all shapes and sizes leap from the head with stylish flair. The hat hoopla, it might be noted, actually started in '09 when Aretha Franklin wore a head statement at the Presidential Inauguration. Since then, the replica has been back-ordered from all over the country. I understand that very hat will be donated to the Smithsonian Institute.

Franklin could haul it off. I would have been arrested for public nuisance.

There are hat people and there are non-hat people. I always admired the hat people. They have large eyes, strong facial features and have a flair for the sublime. They can sweep into a room and pull focus in an awe-inspiring positive way.

You say, "hello, you look so beautiful," and cannot put your finger on why. Ah! The hat, the hat.

If I entered the room wearing a hat, everyone would faint from laughter. Some of us just don't make it when it comes to hats. One of my hag friends says that if she dons a hat, it looks like she's a child playing dress-up with her mother's clothes clomping around in heels five inches too big. Another does not like how they flatten your hairdo, something I wonder about. Did Franklin ever take that hat off to reveal a smashed hairdo, or did she just nail it into her skull right up until bedtime?

And the Queen of England. Does she have an entire castle-addition to store her collection of hats?

When I put a hat on, I become suddenly lost like I had just checked into a tent. I guess it's because my head is too small for a body that is too large.

My head seemed to be a stork's afterthought; the big, dumb body came first and the head was back-ordered. When it came, it was pea-sized, but too late to reorder.

If I were to walk into a store and put on a dressy hat just for fun, the store people along with a few customers would start immediately laughing, then escort me out so as not to scare off business. I guess it's pretty frightening for a headless body to balance a bouquet of flowers.

There are unpleasant hats other than the blooms, bows and bird nests. Some of us have had to wear hardhats while at some job or another. I guess that would prevent death from above by a 300-pound manager accidentally dropping from his desk while studying the bottom line. Death by 300-pound managers is an improved business plan with one less human to pay.

When you remove a hardhat, your skull has morphed into a geometrical configuration that takes hours to breathe into its former self. I once had one on too tight, and my forehead went numb, giving new meaning to the word, "numbskull." Or if it's too loose, it falls backwards when you look up. If you look down, say at your crossword puzzle, it falls thud upon it, leaving your chins to pile up underneath.

In winter months, it is necessary to cover your head with something against the elements. That seems a legitimate excuse to have a hat on, though I take the trash to the curb with a parka hood pulled up and hope that no one sees morning wrinkles which certainly look worse than afternoon wrinkles.

When spring is springing, however, it's hats off for me, breathe the air and hope that my hair flies away without all that hat hoopla.

# The Blame Game

It's always someone else's fault when something goes wrong these days. If we're late, it's because of traffic. If we oversleep, it's because the alarm clock didn't go off. If we make a work mistake, surely it's someone else's fault for not catching it.

And, certainly, if we're too fat, then it must be the fast food industry's fault. Like the guy who took the fast food restaurant to legal task because the high fat content in the menu made him gain weight.

Isn't that sort of like being "over served" at the bar? The bartender must have forced us, kicking and screaming, to glug-glug down too many drinks. For that matter, I should be mad at grocery stores for carrying chocolate. The nerve of them putting temptation too close to my basket so that I would to lose control.

Never mind that this is the information age when studies about health, high fat and just about everything come across in print, internet and television. If you stick your head in the sand, then it's all right to be uninformed and sue someone for getting fat. Or getting cancer from cigarettes.

We've been pointing fingers for a long time, though. As children, there were too many times when minor crimes and mishaps attracted the attention of some parent who had to restore order. Then suddenly, everyone is innocent. There are halos overhead and a barbershop quartet in unison with a harmonious rendition of "not me."

And it's always someone else at fault that "started it." If the boss says I have to work overtime and I clutch my chest and keel over from a heart attack, then I should sue the work place for causing stress in my life. Then I could collect a tidy sum and have a real life.

Hey, I'm getting the idea. Come to think of it, there have been too many missed opportunities from the past when I should have feigned some abuse and pointed a legal finger. When I cheated on a spelling test in the fifth grade, for instance, I should have gotten my parents to sue the teacher for giving me a word that was too hard.

Then, when I didn't make cheerleading, we should have sued the high school for damages to my self esteem. Then, when I got zits, I should have sued all the cute guys for not asking me out because it wasn't my fault that I was ugly.

And here come the genetic predispositions we can blame for a lot of things. It's not just the bartender who over-serves. It's also great-grandfather's third cousin who was an alcoholic and therefore passed down the fateful alcohol gene.

So we inherit zits, allergies and overbites from our ancestors. But whom do we sue if everyone's dead? Maybe the entire medical research field for being slow nitwits by discovering these things too late.

Come to think of it, it's the whole world's fault that I'm a hopeless failure, the lottery's fault that I am unlucky and Mother Nature's fault for wrinkles and sinking body parts. Quick, where's my lawyer?

# A Well-Adjusted Critter Getter

They say, "someone's got to do it" when it comes to jobs that are rather off the beaten path. Never mind the butcher, the baker or the candlestick maker, there have to be morticians and medical examiners around to hold their breath and proceed with what life or death hands them.

My uncle was one such mortician born to fulfill a job that he loved. Family lore says that by the time he was a teenager, he was avidly subscribing to casket magazines. Career-driven to deal with living bodies and dead souls, he loved every minute of his work. And someone had to do it, after all.

I have never met a medical examiner, but there are documentaries about pathologists who regard their living and dead work to be honorable and even enjoyable.

The wild life nuisance remover, or official critter getter, is someone else who says that, "someone's got to do it." But secretly he loves his job and can't wait to get the next hysterical phone call from a terrified female hag about something living or dead in her attic.

I made the call last week when I decided to explore my attic for its renovating possibilities. A friend was with me, so we took on the tour. I rarely go up there because I get the creeps at the mere thought of anything possibly diseased with teeth flying around.

So we opened the stairs door and crept up slowly. I was sure that a ghost of the past would appear from nowhere, say "boo" and "ha ha, you're mother dresses you funny." But then it would get a closer look at me, get scared and disappear without further ado.

We looked around briefly and no ghost, scared or not, appeared. But then my heart stopped. There at my feet was a dead bird. Not just any old dead bird, but a black one whose kissing cousins are ravens, vultures and all things in the world that give you the willies. If it had been a red cardinal, I would have given it a proper funeral and grieved. Or even blue as in blue jay, I'd have forgiven it for its bad reputation that says it is an aggressive, ill-tempered bird.

But the thing was black, so all sorrowful emotions were abruptly cancelled.

Properly aghast, we turned back down the steps. Had I not shouted in time, my friend would have tripped over yet another black bird. My life passed before me.

My original plan was to don surgical scrubs and gloves to sweep various debris onto a sheet and throw out everything. But then there was the queasy stomach factor, so that calls for a critter getter.

When he showed up, he fondly remembered every squirrel, every ground hog and every attic ghost that he exterminated within five blocks. He even named them, like notches on his belt. He stomped around the upstairs fearless of what he may encounter. In fact, he looked forward to a direct confrontation. The ghost appeared, shook hands and told him that he was most handsome.

This same critter getter de-batted a friend's house several summers ago when she called about an errant bat behind the hallway mirror. We hid and shook on the front porch, while he reached behind the mirror and practically said, "Here batty, batty. Here batty batty."

I asked the critter getter how he can stand this line of work. "Someone's got to do it," he said. I know that he secretly loves hysterical hags and fearful ghosts.

# The Cure For Fatal Carpeting

**Y**ou can hate carpeting for only so many years. After that, it becomes a dangerous assault against your physical and mental health. It took me 17 years for the disease to become a raging Level IV diagnosis.

When I first moved into the house, my reaction to the carpeting was in the early stages of discomfort. I could easily ignore it because, after all, it was on the second floor.

So it was a low-priority illness and in denial, I could pretend that Fatal Carpeting didn't exist. There were young children and pets present, anyway, so I could justify not addressing the illness for some years. There will be accidents and spills here and there, so I just tried not to look, hoping that in the future there would be a cure for what ailed me.

I shuddered quietly in those years as I passed over the carpeting from day to day. Some stomach disorder was experienced as I noticed the less-than-designer colors. There was "Bile Green" in one bedroom and "Nausea Yellow" in the hallway and bathroom -- both indoor-outdoor carpeting in its full lack of plush.

But meantime, there were other horrifying offenses to my mental health that had to be treated first. Like the "Halloween Orange" carpet on the first floor covering oak floors. It was surgically removed along with the "Mashed Pumpkin" draperies. For awhile, the color of newsprint in the dining room provided temporary relief medication.

Other decorating diseases had to be treated, as well. The third bedroom had been painted, "Migraine Pink," with layers underneath including, "Mustard Yellow," "Embalmed White" and "Weed Green."

For symptoms of "Painting Over Hardwood" illness, the treatment was more life-threatening than the disease itself. But I survived the effects of the paint stripping chemical fairly unscathed.

But Fatal Carpeting was still festering and rapidly becoming a major illness. I became a babbling idiot when friends visited. If anyone wanted to use the bathroom upstairs, I would fly into a nervous vibration trying to block the stairway.

"Please, don't look down when you go to the second floor," I would beg. I was also mortified to have a guest stay in the "Bile Green" bedroom.

But I still had not enough Fatal Carpeting benefits to treat the disease. So I would have to wait and hope for a magic cure. Meantime, there were other illnesses to treat. Appliance Meltdown required immediate attention as well as a major blood transfusion of the main water line. The water heater required minor surgery. And, of course, there's always the Electrical Outlet Anemia to correct.

My Fatal Carpeting was in remission for a time, but short lived. Finally, one day a massive stroke took me by storm. I could not ignore the symptoms any longer.

The day began normal enough as I decided to switch bed frames in two rooms in order to satisfy a yen for change. One frame had a book shelf that I wanted near an outlet. I set about to dismantle the furniture.

At first, I didn't notice the hyperventilating, but found myself suddenly nauseated. It turned into a desperate situation as I ran for ripping tools to destroy the old carpet beneath. In this dire emergency, I couldn't work fast enough to alleviate my discomfort. Timing was key. I had to race to the carpet store with a measuring tape.

The emergency carpet store people were concerned about my vital signs at first, but as soon as I was able to say, "Quick, where do I sign?" they were relieved to be there for me to recover from "Fatal Carpeting."

# Having the Handy-Dandy Wife on Staff

I apologized to the handyman the other day about my driveway that still looked like Antarctica. He answered by giving me some friendly life instructions that "you should" do this and "you should" do that and, one shovel at a time, my driveway would be a lot better.

I felt my blood pressure rise. First of all, I don't remember asking him how I "should" conduct my life and then if so, I would tell him that one shovel at a time is how I do everything. A sentence here, laundry there, here a dust cloth, there a vacuum and then it's time to get ready for the regular job. One shovel at a time is basically how many of us run our entire lives. Just ask any single mother, divorced or widowed working person.

And did I hear him say that he had a wife? Wife refers to the domestic specialist. Sometimes it is a full time job, but in today's world more often than not happens after another full time job.

I remember my uncle leaning back at the kitchen table after an evening meal, belching and running a toothpick. He patted his stomach with satisfaction and oinked, "What's for dessert?" My aunt, home from her full time day job also, froze with hostility. Her eyes turned into globes as she announced to him that she had worked all day and happened not to have baked a cake.

It reminded me of a work boss recently when a single mother had to call in about a child problem and how she thought the attendance policy too stringent. His chest puffed up into a peacock, his mouth slid sideways and he stood tall and proud. "I've called in only once in the last ten years," he boasted with a swiveling head. He didn't mention it, but had a wife on staff, also. She probably cooks dinner, fixes his lunches and does his laundry. Her calendar is probably full of child maintenance with errands to get groceries and dry cleaning, then have a clean and organized house when he comes home.

Basically, all the work boss does is show up both places where all activities are on autopilot.

It must be a pretty good life to have a wife on staff. I mentioned this to a male the other day and he said, "Oh, I know how to do all that stuff." Then he set out to prove that he once did a load of wash ten years ago and knows how to make an omelet all by himself. Why, he can even get the right stuff at the grocery store. He did that twice when "the wife" was giving birth twenty years earlier.

Then, we're all supposed to cheer about how he actually did the laundry. "He mixed a satin blouse with the bathroom rug, but his heart was in the right place." a friend confided. Another friend said that her husband overloaded the washing machine so much that it developed indigestion and couldn't move through the spin cycle.

Then I hear from various husbands about how they don't like leftovers and get tired of the same thing two days in a row. I always think to myself that if someone cooked for me after a day's work, I wouldn't complain about what was on the menu. "You mean you're eating lasagna every day this week?" a coworker is aghast. Well, I have no wife on staff to make a restaurant-worthy menu complete with specials that reflect the exact mood of every day.

But I didn't mention any of this to the handyman. Sometimes, I "should" keep my mouth shut.

# Designer Furnace Filters and One Inch

I t seems an ordinary thing to do every autumn, but changing furnace filters in my house turns into a complete nervous breakdown. Every year, it seems, I lose and the furnace flexes its ducts with victory.

It is not just having to go to furnace filter stores that is so bothersome, but having to go to furnace filter stores twice in one day. That's when I wonder if my whole life is sometimes on a thankless treadmill looking for a goofy object that measures 24 inches by 15 inches by one.

I have never been an avid store seeker to begin with. Grocery shopping is least interesting to me. The bags are hauled in, consumed, and turned into flab before the dishes are washed. Then you have to do it all over again trying to include the items that you forgot. Specialty stores that sell knitting yarn or artwork, are little more inviting, especially when I need to process various objects I already have. I'd rather spend more time at home with the stuff I already have. Parking lots don't interest me, nor constant pursuit of emptying the checking account into a barrel of dull essentials.

But, no, there is always something else to have to get. My heart sank when I heard the furnace kick on one autumn morning. It was a signal worse than being arrested for wearing white after Labor Day. Or turning in my sandals to look for warm socks. When the heat came on, I knew what was next. It meant two rectangular dumb objects with exact measurements. Once installed, I'll never see them. I will just have the knowledge that cooties will magically fly past me and collect in the basement.

Except I wrote down the dimensions one inch off. That one inch ruined my whole life.

So I probably have the only furnace in the civilized world where the filter slots are exactly twelve inches from the chimney. To replace them, I have to diet off a sudden 20 pounds to shimmy between spider webs and dust to begin by removing the door. Naturally, it won't come out unless I hammer the ugly thing silly and jerk it around with killer vengeance. Neighbors probably think that there's a violent assault next door. Finally off, time to remove the old filters.

This is where trapeze artist skills come in handy. I have to bend down between the gap and around a corner to look into a gaping dark hole and find the slots where the new filters go. It would be handier to be an Olympic-trained octopus with flashlight in yet another hand, but working quickly is necessary before the blood rushes to my head and my body turns into a paralyzed pretzel.

It is not the first time I have had an altercation with my furnace. One year, it sneezed and blew out its own pilot light several times. I think I heard it snicker when the act of relighting was again required by that same octopus. "Hold this button down, light at opposite end three feet away and juggle pennies from the change jar while holding your breath…" is what the furnace instructions said.

Working up a sweat and jostling the new filters around, I finally realized that the new ones would not fit. With my entire blood supply in my head, I noticed the measurements of the old ones. One lousy inch off.

At round number two at the furnace filter store, the checker couldn't seem to fathom my disgust when I asked, "do they come in pink?"

# The Hallmark of Success

I was looking for a birthday card to send to a friend the other day when it occurred to me that the greeting card industry should target more real people in real life situations.

The present selection of cards fills entire aisles with few people in fewer events. The selection assumes that there are no other times in life except those that require lightweight poetry to perfect people prancing around with floral arrangements wearing phony smiles.

Don't get me wrong – I love roses. But there has to be a little manure, also.

My ex-mother-in-law used to devote her entire life to these greeting cards. If no one gave birth, became ill, died, got confirmed, graduated or wed, she couldn't think of anything to do, except perhaps look for dust in my house.

There are other events in life, however, that could be a boon to the entire greeting card industry. "Congratulations," for instance, "on getting your first dead-end job." And the rhymes would explore more of life's little instructions about survival when you leave your brain at the work door.

A sympathy card for your washing machine that died, or a new roof leak might include some poignant rhetoric about looking on the bright side: your furnace and water heater still work.

The greeting card people should tune into other events that need thoughts of kindness. Like automobile words of wisdom that target every episode from a flat tire and dying on the highway to the fateful decision to have to buy a new one. "We are thinking of you," the card would begin, "as you must face your next car loan."

There should be a hormone section of greeting cards that offers condolences throughout all phases of womanhood that include everything from zits to Postpartum Depression. Though it is most encouraging that Shoebox Greetings carries a category of appropriate PMS selections, there still needs to be more attention toward various disorders associated with hormonal changes.

"On this week of swollen ankles, fiery temper and a bloated stomach," the card would begin with appropriate words of sympathy.

Sympathy cards for families stricken with the PMS presence should also be included in the condolences. "Thinking of you at this time of the month," could be directed at spouses and children.

Beyond life events, there are other people to address. For instance, I've been looking for an appropriate card for 20 years without success. I want it to read, "to the person who was rude to me at my own house 25 years ago…" and continue with some prose that hopes, "you get run over by the next truck."

With a nation of so many depressed people, there should be various greetings to serve them. Maybe some Prozac poetry and thoughtful lines about, "viewing the world through black-colored glasses."

There are no greeting cards to include substance abusers like congratulatory cards about completing The Twelve Step program or length of time of sobriety.

Or for dysfunctional families who don't speak to each other. "To my jerk brother-in-law on the occasion of his tenth year of remaining unemployed and worthless," might include an illustration of an unpleasant looking horizontal figure.

To the father-in-law who refused to come to your wedding, there could be "thanks, but no thanks" notes that would sum up your hostility with colorful weapons amidst darkened poetry.'

"Ha ha," reads the card to the professor who flunked me 40 years ago because I didn't seem to "fit in" to grammatical rules and regulations or to the aunt who said that females can't make a living.

It should be "Basher Box" greetings to target everyone in your life that you want to greet in a big way!

# Not a Happy Camper

I hear all kinds of pleasant plans from vacation campers who love to "get away from it all."

Get away from what?

I never understood what is relaxing about working twice as hard for food, clothing and shelter that we already have at our houses. The planning and packing stages to load a pop-up something-or-other would exhaust me more than the regular stuff I have to do when not vacationing.

Or, if I had wanted to mortgage the house to gas up something monstrous and haul freight around the country, I would have gone for truck driver training.

Another point against camping in my book is that the more we try to get away from it all, the more we run into it all. Like each other. Campsites often populate themselves into such close-quartered tenements that open spaces are becoming parking lots with rules.

No, I am not a camper.

My main drawback about choosing to rough it is that I happen to prefer indoor plumbing. We haven't come this far from recorded civilization not to provide flushing facilities in our own homes at a moment's convenience.

Actually, this is not about the institution of the infamous outhouse. Those of us who remember the creaky door and fresh rear-end breeze carry a healthy sense of history remembering that little shack with a moon on the door.

It's the OTHER outdoor facility that bothers me. The one that easily serves males, that is.

"Well, you just…" they shrug and all that is required is one modest-sized bush.

For us, the logistics for the outdoor facility are a bit more complicated.

First is the psychological counseling phase. We must be convinced beyond a reasonable doubt that there is a private thicket deep in the woods where no one will peek. Our entire self esteem would be completely destroyed if anyone, stranger or friend, happened upon this highly irreversible act.

So someone must stand guard.

Next, there has to be a total change of clothes nearby. That is to account for the newly soaked pant leg and a now squishy shoe. (Think about the singular of both.) More psychological counseling is in order at this stage since most of us do not make a habit of changing clothes outside.

So multiply the fresh wardrobe supply and dry shoes by how many times we must use the outdoor facility – I don't have that many clothes to pack.

And yes, I have camped. I had to prove my distaste for the idea some twenty years ago. The promise was that I was required to do no cooking nor washing dishes. I was unimpressed, anyway, with campfire ingredients that consisted of some canned stew with a shelf life into the next millennium and one pathetic fish with more bones than meat. The coffee was somewhere between chewable medication and material to build houses.

Washing dishes was another curiosity, I observed, and most disease threatening using lake water and some abrasive sand. It was probably the same sand particles that found their way into my lumpy sleeping bag. Turning over was like sleeping with a Brillo pad.

I still have nightmares about that same Brontosaurus mosquito that personally stalked me throughout Michigan's Great Lakes.

Yes, I love the sounds of nature. How pleasant are the birds chirping and the crickets cricking. I hear them just fine from the wilds of my front porch. I also see stars twinkling above from there. My refrigerator works just fine with supplies nearby.

And so does my indoor plumbing.

# Tʜe Iɴᴠɪsɪʙʟe Raɪse

It's that little ray of hope in life that we all look for in our paycheck.

If we're lucky enough to have a place of employment, that is, a place that regularly hands out our means to survive. Then the next hope is some reward for our loyalty to an organization.

Then, ah, maybe a few extras in life. Maybe a new car, for instance, or some other wise investments like a more expensive anti-wrinkle cream or new wardrobe of camouflage elastic waistlines.

But I couldn't find my raise recently. The calculator couldn't find it, nor could the fine print on the pay stub.

"Oh yes," a cheerful voice came from payroll, "it's been there for three weeks."

Hmm, that's funny, I thought. I know that I need new glasses prescription, but why does my check look suspiciously smaller than usual? A coworker then advised me that my raise rate should appear in a minuscule corner of the stub.

She took out a microscope. "I see it!" she exclaimed, like she had just discovered DNA.

"No," I told her, "that's where I sneezed just a moment ago."

I gave up asking bosses a long time ago about how the pay raise system works. Mainly because I just don't understand it. Also, I have a nasty habit of reading the "employment" articles in big newspapers where columnists write helpful advice about approaching your company for a raise.

Here's how it goes. You knock politely on the boss door and peek in with forefinger raised. "Have you noticed how brilliant, dedicated, resourceful, organized and well-qualified an employee I am? Not to mention talented and good-looking to have around?"

"Why yes," he leans back, and explains that he was just arranging for a huge raise effective immediately that will put me into a least six figures because I am brilliant, dedicated...

Who negotiates those pay raises? Perhaps an anchor for NBC or an oil company executive.

The rest of us working slobs are at the mercy of the pay raise "system" that doles out cents per century. I once asked a boss to explain it to me. He reached for the employee handbook, an industrial strength calculator and his degree in accounting before he positioned himself at the chalkboard with baton in hand.

He showed me my current rate. It was a lonely figure buried in fine print between percentages, multipliers and dollar-killers.

"Let's see, your start date was..." Clackety clack went the calculator, and pages flipped. The room began to spin.

"And so, we take the hang nail that you had in '03, multiply it by the number of lunar episodes of menopausal behavior. Oh, yes, and subtract the number of your unrelated work conversations and glares at the plant manager in '04. Then we subtract the number of skills you won't have next year because a new machine will eliminate your job, Gobbly Gook, Bibbity Bobbity Boo and rootie toot toot," he clacked away.

I took two aspirin.

He proudly found my raise. "Don't spend it all in one place," he winked.

So why is my check smaller than usual?

"Oh, quite simply, the medical insurance went up," he announced with great pride, and began whizzing around the room to retrieve 50 pounds of insurance books.

When I left, dejected, he was cheerfully explaining that the company had added hang nail insurance multiplied by the bird flu hazards in the air along with post menopausal symptoms that cause the temperature in the work place to elevate global warming.

# THe CoNSUMMate CoUcH

I t was elegant and unassuming in the store. All earthy colors, it looked like it belonged in my house. I deserved it, just like other grownups with couches.

The guys hoofed it in and placed it carefully where I had prepared. Its envelope of creature comforts beckoned as I thanked the movers at the door. I couldn't wait to lounge and read on my newfound luxury.

By the time I got back from the door, two dogs were sound asleep at each end. They looked like canine bookends with happy slits for eyes and Z's drifting upward. Not long after that, I realized that the unassuming couch was equipped with magnets that attracted animal hair. If a cat moseyed through the room minding its own business, the fur suddenly turned into arrows that headed straight for the couch.

Nevertheless, I issued terse pronouncements to my daughter that there would be no food, wrestling or funerals for the buried remote control on the couch. I disappeared for five minutes and when I returned, she was lined up with three friends eating pizza on my new couch. That was ten years ago and since then, the couch has developed its own personality.

At some point, I seriously believed that it had become alive, like the little man in the refrigerator who turns the light off and on. When I was in the room, it had a halo from armrest to armrest. If I pretended to leave, I might catch it in some act. But no such luck; same halo.

The first living couch trait was that it had developed an appetite for all objects within sitting range. Besides the regular assortment of pens, coins and cell phones, it managed to devour a child's retainer. I never found the owner of that retainer, but I am suspicious of that first pizza lineup.

The couch also has an uncanny ability to shuffle objects from the floor to store underneath. Once, I left the room and believed that I heard a satisfying "belch" that it had consumed some important paperwork. Sure enough, when I returned and moved the couch, there was someone's birth certificate, dusty and freshly digested with a few magazines between.

The couch also developed a pharmaceutical ability to dispense tranquilizers as soon as hags sit to read something. Within five minutes, the thing swallows up hags into a fetal shape until there is no longer any sign of life.

Added to the repertoire of this consummate couch is that it happily served as a canine birthing facility. I had prepared a comfy box and blanket on the basement landing for some due puppies, but left and returned to a new happy family, where else? On the couch. A friend has labeled my infamous couch as the one with, "afterbirth and spilt wine."

So I became an expert on every couch cleaning solution possible, but removal of canine afterbirth and teenagers with remotes were never included in the fine print.

I have heard of furniture that looks good and lasts a long time. I think, however, that the owners pretend to use it but rather drape plastic over it. Their living rooms, furthermore, must be protected by Plexiglas and constant emissions of anti-bacterial solutions, and perhaps separated with a velveteen rope so that no one is allowed to live and dwell near the site of the couch.

Those couches must look as handsome as mine did in the store. I worry, however, that the perfect-couch people have nothing to write about or no sinking feeling that the couch won't let them stand up.

# Hot Headed About Cold Feet

Someone asked me recently why I was wearing wool socks during warm weather. The boring answer was that my foot was still numb from a sciatic attack some years ago.

The real answer, however, is that I have not yet recovered from my marriage to a reptile. Actually, I haven't met a married couple yet that can agree on the temperature of anything.

And the dating phase of any relationship does not count. In that era of early lovey-dovey, couples live off the heat of beating hearts and chemical explosions. Then the cooling process happens by gazing at the stars and moon in the sky.

But once there is one thermostat in the household of opposite genders, the battle lines are drawn. My first warning sign was when my husband sweat profusely in the same room that I saw my own breath.

While I always understood that it is healthier to sleep in a slightly cool room, his idea of creature comforts was a fresh layer of snow at the foot of the bed. He preferred that the room temperature was adequate to store a cadaver. If I balked about the house being too cold in the winter, his thoughtful advice was to wrap a nice warm noose around my neck!

And as autumn turned, he wanted to hold the record for the last house in the neighborhood to fire up the furnace. Finally, when I had worn earmuffs and a scarf in the kitchen some days in a row in late October, he said that I should "bake something" to warm up the kitchen. My response warmed up the whole block.

He blamed his aversion to heat on his Swedish ancestry. His homeland skirts the North Pole, I notice. Last year, he had the opportunity to visit distant cousins in Stockholm. I'm sure that they all stood at the shore of the Baltic Sea on the farthest point from land and, with open nostrils, beat their chests in appreciation of hostile elements. Whatever the translation of "ah" in Swedish is probably what they said.

Some generations later in the Midwest, he still admires a weather condition that looks more like a shipwreck outside and arthritis inside. "Ah," he gazes through the windowpane while a frozen gray rain pelts against the windows. "What a gorgeous day!"

He also must have the fans on the highest and noisiest speed. It felt much like living in a wind tunnel. One control button and anything not nailed down sailed across the room including loose papers and small children.

No Swedish immigrant to date has settled further south than Michigan or Minnesota. The Chicago area for my ex-husband is far too south for him. He sweats and suffers when most of us enjoy a perfectly wonderful day. In fact, I often wondered why he didn't volunteer to be the first official ridiculous person on staff for the wintering crew in Antarctica.

This reptilian kind of bloodstream also flows in my son. He and I visited Maine one Thanksgiving for his first experience on an ocean coast. With a faraway look in his eyes, he stood on wave-beaten rocks to bond with the coldest Atlantic. I sat bundled in the car and took aspirin.

The car is also a temperature conflict. When my ex-husband visits to go out to dinner with friends, I have to prepare for the six-block drive to the restaurant. Basically, I dress for a hayride. If it is a cold day, he opens all the windows for "fresh air." If it's a warm day, there are icicles forming on the air conditioning and an ongoing litany about "whoever invented hot weather should be shot."

# Pick a Storm, Any Storm

If it's a new day, it's a new storm. Mother Nature needs to up Her dose of Prozak these days. She is a roller coaster of different moods that make it confusing just to part the curtains and see what She's doing today.

On a particular winter day before Christmas, there was a brutally cold and windy spell. I was determined, however, to get across town for the Second Annual Hag Exchange with my friends, below zero wind chill or not. So I arranged to pick up one friend along the way. A normally ten-minute buzz across some city blocks turned into an epic with several chapters. I gave her cell phone updates;

"OK, I'm chipping the ice and warming the car, now – it started, but groaned and oinked and stood in the garage defiant. I think it tried to bargain with me and promise a million miles if I leave it alone tonight to cozy up next to the lawnmower...

"OK, I'm at the gas station now prying open the tank cover (bang bang), the pump doesn't want to pump nor print out a receipt. I'll have to go inside but I can't find my mittens and the wind is (whirrrr)...

"OK, I'm on your street now, but the car still isn't warmed up. I think it's still mad about leaving the garage..." And thus a half hour later, we were still in transit feeling like we were weathering the maiden voyage in some ship's journey to Antarctica.

The next day, temperatures rose, but just in time for the first of three snow storms rolling in like blizzards. There were cell phone updates all around as family and friends gathered for an Eve dinner and general hoopla.

"OK mom, we just left and ah, I better go because we can't see the road..." And the snowflakes got larger, then smaller, then horizontal.

227

Within the next 48 hours, there were several cars, including mine, that got stuck with that familiar sound of rocking the car to and fro. That's when the males burst out of the house in single file, almost gleeful that there was a problem to solve. The pecking order was that the oldest male with the most heart attacks came first. Passing him up was a son-in-law wearing a Superman cape and flexing his muscles. Hum-drumming last in line and least interested was a perfectly fit black-belted Karate son, limping to favor his back that he'd thrown out earlier while shoveling.

But alas, Superman swept his cape into the driver's seat and saved the day!

And the next few days piled up more with some freezing rain condition layering the precipitation effect.

Within one day, the thermometer roller-coasted to a blazing 55 degrees. The piled snow turned into floods, rivers rose and I think I saw Noah's Ark paddling down the street. At every turn of cable updates, there were "breaking news" reports blinking red to update some weather disaster or another around the country.

This is all very confusing, of course, when you try to decide what jacket to wear. You may start out with a robust down parka with hood and scarf first thing in the morning. By lunch, you may be scaling down to denim wear and by dinner, a full sea-diving wetsuit.

A friend and I decided to do a shopping trip for the sales. "What's the weather supposed to be?" she wondered.

"Well, first an ice storm followed by sleety rain, then flooding. I believe there's a tornado warning by evening ." She rolled her eyes, "whatever."

# The Life and Times of Cooties

I was recently at two occasions where a person or two wore a face mask to protect themselves from infamous flu viruses in the midst.

I found it mindful and responsible to care for personal health on one hand, but otherwise had other ideas about current and fashionable cooties these days.

My first experience with cooties was in the third grade when the fad was making "cootie catchers," out of notebook paper. It was sort of like Origami weaponry, no less threatening than any ordinary spit ball designed to give you the creeps from the boy with a cowlick next door.

But then more menacing cooties came along. They used to be relatively innocuous individuals swirling about with no other agenda but to fell a human here and there, especially one who might not be in the mood for the day job. "I have the flu, (ah, er, cough, cough), oh gosh, I had better not come in today."

Or, "Gee, I am suddenly ill (sound of tinkling glasses and music band in background), I think I had better stay away and recover." Just academic research, of course.

Those cooties kept their day job for years and made no impact on the Center for Disease Control. There was a cootie for sniffles, one for sore throats and one that attacked hags with several chins. Teens got zit cooties, seniors got Charley Horse cooties, mothers got cooties from saying "No!" every five minutes. Cooties here, cooties there and none of them had the strength for any impact.

Then cooties got organized. Their new union grew into slick Cootie Corporate, and smarter all the time.

The Cootie Corporate Ladder has a long history of ups and downs, fits and starts, sneezes and coughs. I remember when the Hong Kong flu came to town. Everyone had their own personal story about that cootie invasion. There were statistics all over about how many couldn't report to work, how many were missing from the news stations and how many simply came home and fell out for weeks. And those cooties took up residence and hung on seemingly forever.

But then, Cootie Corporate broke into splinter groups, some dysfunctional, some weaker and some extremists that couldn't find a proper place in society.

It seems during that disorganized time, co-workers had this idea that cooties had personal name tags. If I blew my nose at work and someone else got sick, then I was immediately blamed because I wore Polka dots or colors that didn't match that day. And they could prove it because they witnessed arrows with jeering teeth and black hats emitting from my pink Kleenex toward everyone else to cause illness. Yup, it was my personal cooties all along.

Those were the days when calling in sick was a crime, but showing up was also. Darned if you do; darned if you don't.

But now cooties have again organized into a much stronger Corporate mission. The Cootie Company Handbook states that everyone, even those without Polka dots and colors that don't match, are susceptible using bar code name tags. The fine print says something about "equal opportunity" bylaws, including hags with stomachs that stick out.

It's a cootie takeover again. People can't help looking askance at the person beside them and wondering if that is a dreaded cooties carrier with jeering teeth and black hats.

Old habits die hard, however. I couldn't help thinking that perhaps I was wearing the wrong outfit and had the wrong color Kleenex when a man in front of me glared through his mask.

# FaSHioNS For tHe Derriere Crevice

I was standing in line at the store the other day when I realized that I was counting fruit on someone's underwear.

His hat was backwards, of course, but that didn't strike me as peculiar. After all, it's been a long time since men actually took off their hats when they entered a dwelling. Removing hats is in the same category as picking up a dropped handkerchief or spreading a jacket over a puddle. Chivalrous gestures went out with the Edsel. These days, women are lucky to have the door held for them rather than slammed shut because he is busy texting his girlfriend, the one who doesn't like his cell phone habits.

Youthful fashions have always come and gone quickly, but this one about the pants falling down seems to linger. I can't imagine why because it would seem highly inconvenient to walk down the street and constantly hike up one's pants. I've seen at least 15 hikes per hopscotch measurement, and sometimes more.

If the fad is strong, I wonder about the shopping trip to buy those oversized guaranteed-to-fall-down pants. The skinniest dude must hold XXL pants to his waist and if there is at least a foot to spare on either side, "that'll work," he says. If he tries them on, the pants must pass the fall-to-the-floor speed test.

Then a trip to the underwear department is in order to feature the derriere crevice section of the cool dude costume. There must be a proper selection of fruit, Polka dots and stripes. Boxers or briefs? No, just elastic that insures hanging-out plumage.

The cool dudes are not the first who wanted their underwear public. Mini skirts revealed all including a complete repertoire of body parts with some adipose tissue thrown in. The skirt at least stayed in place, so there was no derriere display, but I think it became too much work to sit comfortably. Either that, or there was simply too much adipose tissue on display. We got over that one quickly!

I was a bit too anxious to push the fashion mini-skirt envelope because my high school principal once threatened to send me home. My skirt was too short and somehow I escaped my house in the morning without notice. I was so petrified about my parents grounding me that I promised him I wouldn't wear it again. At least I was thin in those days.

We also had sewn-down pleated skirts in high school – yes that certainly dates me – and I became so sick to death of them that I cut them into strips for a braided rug. I never finished the project because I was sick to death of that, also. I notice that the pleated fashion has never returned successfully since. I once stood at a rack that displayed a few pleats for a test comeback and became so nauseated that the manager gently escorted me from the store.

The mini, maxi and midi come and go, also. Some say that the hemlines go up and down according to the nation's economic health. After the mini, however, my hemline stayed down. It had nothing to do with economic health. It was my own health when I looked in the mirror.

Then, of course, bell-bottoms, or the fashion that became the most popular Halloween costume in recent times. That seemed a style quickie that came and went along with tie-dyed T-shirts.

So if tl.e derriere dudes become tired of hiking up their pants, they could look equally as ridiculous with bells and tie-dyes, without all that extra work.

# The Next Generation of Zeroes

They're saying that our children and grandchildren will inherit the national debt that we currently pass along.

The economic raised forefingers probably secretly hope that we will be safely spinning in our graves before that happens. For now, we grownups have a disastrous credit situation, and are helpless to fathom what to do next.

In other words, if you lay all the zeroes of debt from end to end, they will reach the moon and back several times before they orbit the ATM machines.

This as I was getting a handle on the nice look of six zeroes in a million dollars. With gouging eyes of jiggling green, I would look up to millionaires like they were enviable with all their riches and wealth. They had big important check books wide enough for all those zeroes. "If I were a millionaire…" I would dream.

But now I'm hearing that those marvelous six zeroes amount to "paltry," "only" and "a drop in the bucket." So as an established twenty-aire, I guess those fat zeroes are skinnier than I thought.

That shows you that I know zero about zeroes. The only other zeroes I remember had to do with feeling like one. Like when the cute boys never noticed me in the fifth grade when I wore the latest and hottest sack dress. Then the same cute boys grew into high school hoods that always flirted with the popular girls, not me with my zits and zero self esteem.

"How many guys asked you to the prom, Sue?" Oh, try zero.

Then comes the alphabet soup of zeroes. I was discussing how many zeroes were in a billion with a "b" the other day with a co-worker. He started by saying, "well you can have 100 million," then already got confused when I offered that it's somewhere beyond that at about a thousand gazillions or so. The zeroes were buzzing around his head when I also mused that there are actually some people who are worth billions with a "b". Some rob Peter to pay Paul and live in mansions to tell it, but others actually work for it.

Then another co-worker brought up the trillion with a "tr". He took out a calculator as wide as an ironing board. Both zero-counting co-workers had figures buzzing around their heads when my eyes glazed over. I was rather thinking about how the next generations will process all those zeroes.

Actually, I don't think that they will. First, you would have to unplug them from whatever they're plugged into. "National debt? Never heard of it. Is that a new group?" Another young person says about her car radio, "as soon as I hear talking, I switch the station." So much for knowing what the word, "budget" is.

My daughter defers the household budget to her husband. All the zeroes she needs are enough to get her hair done and order frilly things from catalogues. My poet son only knows zeroes about how many times he has been published.

The generation after that is young yet, but I suspect that they'll just hit the "delete" button because too many zeroes will clog up their PCs and blackberries.

Meantime, inflation will calmly overtake the next generations.

"Can I borrow $10,000 for the coffee machine?" "Hey, man, I just loaned you $20,000 the other day."

And the pockets will get deeper yet, but only because they will accommodate a thick wad of bills and credit/debit cards to make a run to the store for toilet paper.

But it won't bother the next generation of zeroes.

# The Stats Are In

A work cohort flapped an article from the paper in front of my face the other day.

He had that look about him that said, "ha ha, I'm right and you're wrong." It was supposed to be the definitive answer, complete with multiple-digit statistics, about why my opinion on a subject that we had discussed previously was wrong. Never mind that the source of stats was printed from the Shady Press with researchers fresh from the University of "Mad Magazine."

I guess I was supposed to lie down, roll over and cry, "uncle."

But instead, I glanced at the first two sentences and announced that anyone can manipulate statistics. He walked away in a huff mumbling that I, "wasn't reading right."

Statistics have always been a highly interpretive art form. During the Vietnam War, for instance, the reported numbers of lives lost weekly were predictably skewed. The enemy lost four digits, the saving-from-Communism country lost three digits and the Americans lost two digits.

If it's about digits, one can deduce just about anything anytime. A teacher friend agonizes that it is possible to put together some slippery numbers that indicate that class size has no proven effect on the quality of education. That depends on whose side you're on. Teachers, parents, students and the rest of the world claim the smaller, the better. But elusive administration elsewhere and its staff bean counters can create numbers to support the larger class size.

And numbers can be stretched like rubber to self-serve an opinion. I might decide, for instance, that there are X number of people with black hats who commit murders. And there are also X number of people with white hats that commit murders. But those with white hats also eat more carrots. Therefore, it is healthier to commit murder while eating carrots and also see the victims better. Case closed.

For that matter, the number of dysfunctional families seems to out-number the Beaver Cleaver families. But that statistic varies by how one defines a dysfunctional family. The dysfunctional family researcher might compile the per-day number of glares, tantrums and slamming doors. Then factor in how many times a member of that same family smiles in public and asks a saccharine-sweet, "and how are you today?" with a polyester happy-face.

Actually, that study might show that the majority of us are psychotic, never mind the dysfunctional family.

Other studies might show that the room temperature rises by 2.5 degrees when there are more than two menopausal hags per square foot. But the temperature suddenly plunges when one arrogant male walks in. So if the census takers report that there are presently more menopausal hags on the earth than arrogant males, then the polar ice melting will approach faster than previously thought. Unless, that is, the hags are served expensive wine and semi-sweet chocolate. Then no one cares about arrogant males.

Health studies are handy with statistics. If one drinks coffee, for instance, studies might show that there are more jitters at the computer keyboard, thus affecting the Gross National Product in the work place. If the worker stops jittering to think, and the price of the coffee bean rises, then a recession occurs because there is no input and nothing going on. Therefore, thinking on the job while drinking coffee is not recommended.

While the stats keep coming, I have a handy calculator that proves, without a doubt, that I'm right about whatever I want to be.

But the most important statistical studies to date should reveal how many hags are on the head of a pin.

# IF tHe SHoe FitS...

**...b**uy two, so goes the quip. The trouble is, the shoe never fits. And I have a lifetime of trying to prove it.

At the store, the shoes that you try on float above the floor as you whip around the aisle choreographing full length ballets in that marvelous and trendy footwear. "Wrap them up," you tell the shoe store person and hurry home to continue the ballet. The moment you walk into the house, the very shoebox you carry turns conspiratorial. Some wicked step-sisters show up and no handsome prince. You use a tire iron to get them on again while corns and blisters throb and ache. The shoes have suddenly turned two sizes too small.

Sure I love the ornate sandals in the summer and lightweight leather in the winter in all kinds of flashy or earthy colors. But they just don't fit.

High heels don't even count. The last time I even pretended to wear anything higher than the first floor was during the cork wedges in the '70s. The shoes were at least engineered to stand and walk with some degree of safety. The Stiletto heels then and now that take a stepladder to mount are not even in my closet radar. I have too much fear of heights to consider them. Between high heels and skyscrapers; the second floor of my house is the limit.

I once took a fancy to some stylish heels to wear to some function or another. They were foxy suede with an ankle strap to show off various standing positions at a cocktail hour. Luckily, I made it in without anyone noticing my wobbly entrance. The rest of the night, I stood holding onto something to steady myself. But I nevertheless pretended that I was a magazine cover pose.

The first problem is the shape of the foot of normal Homo sapiens. I don't fall into that category. My arch is high enough to drive a semi truck through. My foot print looks like five small dots, one large circle and a connecting bridge. When they talk about arch support, I'd have to stuff the whole Dr. Scholl display into my shoe.

I notice now that pointed toes are returning, a trend that always shocks me. I just can't understand why anyone would want to enter a room with weapons cocked for armed conflict from the ankle down. And suffer discomfort to boot. I doubt that anyone's foot on planet Earth is shaped like a funnel.

When I was little, there were shoe store X-ray machines thought to be an aid to see how new shoes affected our feet. I used to look down at my image with great wonder. But the stage of future shoe-buying was set right then and there when my ghostly foot looked up along with the wicked stepsisters peeking around each bone, conniving and rubbing their palms. Nothing would ever fit and there would be no handsome prince.

Luckily those X-ray machines were deemed health hazards. I think I know why.

I also remember that along with, "back to school" supplies were the infamous Oxfords. I never did figure out the theory about them as a school asset. Maybe they lasted longer. Maybe they were supposed to look academic. Maybe it was a parental conspiracy to make us developing teens look dorky so that our wayward hormones could be controlled a bit longer. Oxfords were also the shoes where those pesky socks would ride down into the ankle, a most annoying way to go "back to school."

They didn't fit, either, but nothing ever does.

# The World's Newest Profession

Not to be confused with the oldest one, of course. But a profession that we badly need to fix our economy; a professional shopper.

And not just any old shopper who clips coupons and makes the routine grocery run. A true professional is certifiably addicted and salivates at the mere sight of a sale sign. The qualified shopper or shoppette views store windows with a racing pulse that can only be calmed by entering and affectionately stroking merchandise.

When the store people see the professional shopper or shoppette coming, they stumble over each other to be the first to say casually, "May I help you?"

"Oh, I'm just…" and the group of clerks clatter in unison to follow the shopper or shoppette trying to get a handle on a nose that goes up and down with trained designer judgment. There are some shoppers that just need to go out and shop for something every day because of the pleasant smell of new merchandise when it arrives home.

But there are others that take the profession seriously enough to train their noses to smell a designer label from across the room.

One of my hag friends is carefully crafting her resume to qualify as an award-winning shoppette. I figure that she will single-handedly save the economy by next week. Maybe sooner.

She stalked a high-end purse for a month. But upon closer examination, her nose wrinkled with, "ugh, the fabric isn't exactly right. It won't match my new red car."

She doesn't bother wasting time with a "hello" when she enters a room. She rather rattles off the list of what she "needs" in her life. The list usually includes various life essentials like a gismo that bakes cookies by remote control. She also fancies high end yarn from Alpacas that she knows personally and includes in her address book as "Frances," "Freddie" and "Florence." But then she remembered one day that she needs to learn how to knit. No matter. The yarn awaits with bits of straw to verify authenticity.

I once knew a snob shopper whose affinity for pure-bred cats affected his friendship with us low-class stiffs. He didn't want his cats to mingle with my cats because his cats would put noses in the air to ask, "And where are your parents?"

There are other shoppers who venture out to look for things that they need. I learned a long time ago to avoid stores between paychecks. That way, I can exercise control over my "needs." Like queenly clothes fit for clotheshorses when I get them home and suddenly remember there are no events to wear them to. And shoes that I can't wobble across the room in nor remember what I bought them for.

But the stores come to you sometimes in the form of catalogues. They're always juicy to look at for the moment. In order to exercise control, however, I stack them with dog-eared pages that say, "later." The last time I checked, that stack of catalogues nearly reached the ceiling with those "later" notes.

So I guess that my resume for the world's newest profession stands at zilch right now. I won't be able to save the economy any time soon.

But there are always hag friends available for me to enjoy a vicarious experience of their shopping escapades. The last time I checked, one of them was scheming her next purchase of a jacket for each and every Fahrenheit degree above zero. Then, of course, there will have to be shoes to match and a personal Alpaca scarf to boot – as soon as she learns how to knit.

# There's No Place Like Home

Every now and then I like to visit open houses for sale just to browse and see what's out there.

By the time I looked at two houses nearby, I was ready to hire an arsonist for my own. I came home to inefficient use of space, bedrooms too small and a most lowly kitchen.

Then I wondered how it is that everyone else can suddenly elevate themselves to the HGTV channel seemingly without budget constraints. My house is surely the only one in the world that needs an upgrade. I never even noticed that house down the street and now suddenly I need to gather funds, give blood and beg the real estate lady to accept my offer of unemployment paperwork and a 25-cent pension.

So a friend came over and read the spec sheet of that neighboring house. While I clutched my throat and seethed at the very sight of my own walls, she assured me that my house was most presentable and that I should be content with what I have.

To prove her wrong, I took her down the street with me. She drooled in every room, looked with lust at a charming reading nook and imagined herself happily entertaining and living comfortably for the rest of her life in the very house that she snubbed five minutes earlier.

"Did you see how wonderful the deck is?" she was starry-eyed. "The kitchen?" "The porch swing?" she went on.

"Have you called that arsonist yet?" she asked on the way back. Then she did a U-turn and snuck back to make an offer on the spot. Last time I looked, she was hovering in front stalking the seller, clicking her heels and saying, "there's no place like home."

While I am not quite ready for the arsonist, I notice too many changes in house fashion since 25 years ago when I bought my own. The most notable is that walls have come down in favor of the open-floor plan. I've been trying to tear down walls in the last ten years or so but so far, all I can accomplish is making a mess. Not to be outdone by my daughter who came home from the hospital with a newborn to a pile of plaster where the kitchen used to be located.

Her husband was in the remodeling process, but timing was woefully off. I think that she personally invented the term, "post-partum depression." The walls took note and wondered from then on about that marriage made in heaven.

So the real estate lady, most anxious to sell the house, wondered if I would be interested in selling my own. Then we had a discussion about "disclosure," or full admissions of any house issues I might have.

"Well, er, the toilet nearly fell through the ceiling two years ago," and I was ready to say that all was happily fixed, but she immediately ushered me out the door, but not before she demanded her business card back. I was about to tell her that it was on my list to plaster over a hole in the upstairs bathroom and that the pet stains on the front room rug were in the ammonia process.

"Don't ever call me again," sniped the lady. I guess she didn't want to hear about the water that used to seep into the west wall before I treated the foundation with heaps of compost, or that mice respectfully stay away only because of a hunting housecat named, "The Wicked Witch."

I am now clicking my heels and reconsidering the engagement of arsonist services.

# Toys 'R Them

**W**hen I make my list and check it twice during the holidays, I have no toy stores on it.

There's the grocery, the cute gift shoppe with two "p"s and an "e," the catalogues that pile up and the store with the best German white wine that goes with turkey. But never a toy store.

There's something about them that raises my blood pressure at the door. Maybe it's the Appalachian Mountains of plastic or the Gross National Product tied up in beeps and bongs of battery-driven toys. Or the plethora of products that ensure obliteration of all brains cells of every child born in the Third Age.

Whatever happened to…I can't even remember what toys used to be like! I remember very few actual gifts at Christmas. We weren't poor, but there just wasn't a shower of material things.

In fact, there just weren't many material things out there. I got some treasured doll that I carried for years until it turned into a saliva-infested rag. I also memorized, "Twas The Night Before Christmas" from some fairy tale anthology that I still have on the shelf.

And speaking of shelves, the shelf life of today's toys stands at about five minutes, or whenever the batteries die. Or when some grownup gets lost in inch-thick directions that say in 23 languages those dreaded words "some assembly required."

I think what soured me on toy stores is the expression "I want." And if there's a handy tantrum that follows, I'm done shopping. If either of my children uttered the question, "Mom, can we get…?" one time too many, we headed for the car. And somehow they grew up without all the plastic, beeps, and batteries. As babies, they found alternative toys. One was thrilled to empty the bottom cupboards and bang the pots and pans into nerve-wracking heaven. The first time my daughter crawled, she headed straight across the kitchen floor to the potato bin and systematically threw them, one at a time, over her shoulder as fast as she could. After that, the house turned into one big disassembling project.

Her dad took her to a mega toy store one year when he was feeling most benevolent. His daredevil instructions were that she could have anything she wanted. Then he stood back and quaked in fear that she would choose the most expensive thing she could find that would be beyond the budget.

She deliberated long, and finally chose an inexpensive Barbie Doll. After that, her yearly desires from Santa Claus were a set of paints and an artist's pad -- ten dollars tops.

Now here comes the grandson and what to put on my list and check it twice. I try to fend off an avalanche of plastic and beeps, if possible. Let alone television screens everywhere. Someone gave him a toy recently to gaze at while he wiggles around waiting to learn more important things – like destroying the house. I cannot for the life of me figure out the purpose of this toy. It's a round thing, and when you switch it on, it says, "Whizz, BANG! Rat-a-tat-a-tat!" while several lights flash on and off.

"It stimulates the brain," my daughter says with one of her infamous squiggley-lined smirks that travel to her ear when she thinks her mom is a dork.

"How about reading a book?" I gently suggest. Well, she cautioned me, he'll just throw up on the pages.

"Well, how about putting his little fingers on the piano keys?" He'll throw up on them, too.

Maybe that's why everything is plastic these days.

# 'May Day' For the Flowerholic

I'm not the only one crying for help.

Some of us carry an addictive secret year around without much trouble. But when the calendar suddenly turns to May, I, for one, fall off the flower wagon. If there are two blades of grass left in the yard, I must immediately dig them up to put in a new perennial, annual, bulb or anything that promises a splash of blooms. If I go to the store for Sunday's paper, I return with flats of flowers and an abused checkbook. I might remember the paper.

I notice that I'm not the only one with the problem. I have a friend who took a flashlight in the night to her front yard to clip back a perennial the exact moment she read that spring was the time to do it.

I feel it coming on in the last week of April. Things are flying out of the ground with perhaps a minor snow or frost setback. Once May strikes, however, a mutual garden addict and I have code phrases on the phone.

"OK. They're open on Sunday now," she announces with trepidation from the side of her mouth. "What's the plan?" she whispers. Let's do it, I respond, and my credit card is ready. I tell her to hurry before I start shaking. She has already reported the drive-by inspections. From the curb, she reports that the colors are correct, but prices may be too high for flats of impatiens at that particular nursery.

As partners in crime, we gasp in unison as we near the next plant nursery. The hint of colors brings about an anxiety attack. Then we cruise the selections and inspect each plant as if the decision of a lifetime.

I know that flowerholics come from a genetic predisposition. It skipped a generation in my family since my mother thinks all living things are "messy." So while she cleaned, my grandmother used to sneak me seeds

251

in the mail to plant in my bedroom window. She was also still digging around her petunia patch in her mid-nineties. I relive the story every May that her spirit is following me around the nursery.

"Sue Anna," says her spirit about hollyhocks, "you can just stick them anywhere."

In her honor, I kill a geranium or two every year just to remind her that she was the last one in the family who could get them through dormancy over the winter.

When it's not May, some of us suffer the addiction all winter. My indoor plant collection tends to be a minor forest. I would never have a house, for instance, without sunny windows. I once had a giant-leafed philodendron that would slap my husband in the face when he entered the room. Then there was the infamous corn plant I inherited from a friend that tried to grow through the ceiling. I moved it to the stairwell where it could find its way up to the second floor ceiling.

"What are you going to do when it outgrows that ceiling?" a friend wondered.

Why, cut a hole to the attic, of course. Either that or buy a bigger house. Alas, it sailed to the floor from it own weight and had to join the compost heap.

But there's something about the month of May. I have attempted all kinds of controls for my flower behavior. One includes a firm rule that I'm not allowed to buy more than I can plant in the same day. But what if all the double-bloomed impatiens are gone by tomorrow? Never mind, I had better buy the entire stock today.

We flowerholics are easy to spot these days. We're the ones with leaves flapping out the back seat windows of speeding cars in a hurry to rush home and plant.

# Uncorking the Truth

**N**ot that I pour too much wine or anything, but my corkscrew fainted and died the other day from exhaustion. The side arms went upward like the top of a jumping jack, then one broke. It stood like the Statue of Liberty for a moment before it fell over and expired on the kitchen counter.

I had to fish through the utility drawer to find another one. The last one I used was a bit unreliable. Properly centered and squiggled downward was no problem, but then you had to prop your feet on the wall red-faced and count to ten with obstetrics staff all around. Maybe you would give agonizing birth to a cork, or maybe you would have to take it to a neighbor who lifts weights.

I did that once when a friend and I couldn't get the cork out. We were at least happy that my muscled and macho neighbor also had to struggle with a red face. Then there is the hazard that the cork would implode into pieces in the bottle for a recommended daily requirement of fiber. I've done much expectorating (spitting) at formal occasions because of that.

To make matters worse, they seem to be changing the material of cork so that it is no longer cork anymore. It's more like a material that hugs the bottle for dear life just so that hags who lie about wine consumption can't pour, "just one glass." The new material might be an invention since the '70s when the cork industry was diverted into shoe wedge fashions.

The corkscrews are also on the high-tech rise. My daughter has one that looks like a new-fangled sculpture for a mechanic's alphabetized tool collection. I've even seen some novelty corkers that are designed to trick the imbiber, sort of like a Rubik's cube brain teaser. No thanks; there are enough unpleasant challenges in life.

So I was having a discussion about wine with friends the other day. One said that she tried not to go to the same store two days in a row so that the checker wouldn't look askance at her wine habit.

"Oh, I don't have wine everyday like that," I snubbed. By the time I finished the sentence, my nose grew about a foot. It was the same length as another friend who said that she could eat just one cookie. Maybe they saw us at a store – me with an industrial-strength dolly to cart home a wine supply and her cruising the bakery.

"Well, maybe just one glass," I added. I didn't mention that the glass was the size of a goldfish bowl. I tried to trick myself into a small champagne-sized stem once but the path back and forth to the kitchen wore into a marathon track.

I think that we all misrepresent ourselves when it comes to various habits that get us through. A 94-year-old acquaintance said that she couldn't sleep one night and was most disgusted that she didn't have the strength to uncork the wine bottle. She suddenly changed the subject, however, when her glaring daughter entered the room. That would be the same person who eats, "just one cookie."

And any excuse will do. I operate on the "point system." If I have been a Goody-Two-Shoes that day and have completed some responsible chores, say one load of laundry and a boring phone call for a dental checkup – then I deserve that "one glass of wine."

Or if I chop vegetables and rattle some pans, well, everyone knows that you cannot cook without a glass of wine nearby!

# The Work-At-Home Fantasy

"Work at home!" That's what the posted signs say all around town. Or the invasive computer pop-ups and spam advertisements for making thousands of dollars in less time than it takes to blow your nose.

I have always been suspicious of those EZ money-making deals. In fact, one valuable piece of advice that I have given my children while growing up was that if it seems too good to be true, than it probably is. That includes easy money-making scams and way-too-charming suitors that might be serial killers or sweetheart swindlers in disguise. Or maybe the drop dead attractive gold digger woman that runs your credit into the morgue.

But I can still dream about working at home. It has always had its appeal. I see myself starting the day with a steaming cup of coffee and looking out at the winter storms without having to face them. I could wear my bathrobe all day, or if I really wanted to dress up, wear sweat pants and wool socks.

That's how I imagine that best-selling novelists live. Their office is set up near a designer window with a scenic view of a calm forest. As they clack away brilliant passages with pipe puffing at each paragraph, a deer might appear from the trees and frame a perfect setting for a short break to appreciate all things beautiful in this world. And all is perfect and peaceful in the world of working at home.

But in my life, I can see it now. Whenever I have done any work at home in the past, the house has always interrupted with the annoying din of reality. The throbbing washing machine. The squeaking brakes of the garbage truck. A while back, I was talking to a person that I didn't know, so I tried to act professional, as if I had a desk, office and a life. At that exact moment, the only place in the entire house that my cat wanted to perch was on the very piece of paper that I was trying to write notes on.

Another time, I was trying to leave a message on someone's answering machine, again trying to speak professionally. Here's how it went:

"Hi, Sue Langenberg calling and (bark, bark) blah blah blah (bark, bark) ALL RIGHT, LAY DOWN! blah blah blah."

There are other hazards to working at home for me. If the house interruptions don't interrupt, then temptations tempt. The noon movie about murder and intrigue comes on, so why not do my work during the commercials? Then my stomach growls louder than my thought process, so I had better take a break for lunch. Oops, the cupboards are bare, so I had better go to the store after the murder movie.

Meantime, the mail arrives with my gardening magazines, gift catalogues and knitting fashions. So I abandon my work during murder commercials and lust over the magazines. While I do that, my daughter calls to hyperventilate about some in-law that she can't stand and how she is never going to attend some event or another in that family. I get tangled up in that conversation and worry that I'm missing my murder movie and catalogues. My stomach is growling louder.

Then, there's always that beckoning couch for a quick nap to recover from the phone and all the other interruptions. At this point, I have long since forgotten about my work. The computer has gone into screen saver and promises that my work is worthless, anyway.

I think that I had better keep my day job.

# The Nursing Home Swans

They say that swans mate for life. My question is, just exactly how long is their life?

Not that I am a cynic about the happily-ever-after idea or anything, but I am wondering if these lovey-dovey birds ever experience PMS, mid-life crises, teenagers or menopause. Do they agree on pond politics and swan raising? I wonder if Mrs. Swan has stretch marks from her long-ago egg laying, or if Mr. Swan belches from overeating fish. Or, do they still love each other after his feathers fall out or her swan-in-laws claim she is not graceful enough for the ballet "Swan Lake?"

For some reason, we like to socially engineer ourselves into any lofty mores that come along. If a marriage between swans actually sustains an admirably long life together, than so should we. At least that's what the wagging fingers of fickledom try to tell the doubting Langenbergs.

I notice that our lifespan a century ago was markedly shorter. The gravestones frequently etched a 40-something lifespan in the pre-antibiotic age. Deadly cooties came, and went, leaving a trail of infectious diseases that took lives younger. We have improved our health now, and increased our life span tremendously.

So it would seem logical that by age 40-years-old, the yester-century marriages were already at the "death do us part" stage.

These days, we're just getting started at that age. Our mate-for-lifetime idea may encompass many very long decades of marriage-keeping. First, there's the intrigue-at-first-sight hook. For the women, that means there's a cute guy combing his hair just right and smirking just so. The men at this stage see the pre-hormonal, pre-varicose veins, pre-stretch marks and pre-gravity era hot number. This stage lasts less time than the wedding cake at the reception.

259

The honeymoon is short also and lasts only as long as he puts machine parts on the kitchen counter and she wants a flower garden instead of his workshop. The money arguments promptly begin and cause marital strife. Then she must spend too much money on having her hair done or shopping for new shoes. He thinks that a paycheck is for buying man toys and not for those highway robbers that provide heat and electricity.

The raising children stage is next. That's when he changes one diaper and says peek-a-boo a few times, then brags for the next 18 years about how he should be, "father of the year." The contests about who does more work each day begin. He claims that he slaves at his job for a living, and she claims that she slaves around the house.

With all due respect to young parents everywhere, the raising children stage is the toughest test of a marriage. If both survive the drool on the shoulder, throw-up anywhere, toddler destruction, adolescent and teenage turmoil all while making a living, the swans have nothing to brag about.

When the empty nest comes about, the marriage is like being thrown from a turbulent orbit to a sudden and piercing peaceful existence. As the dust settles and bifocals adjust, there is a new test. No more slick talk and wavy hair days. The chins fall, the stomach juts and the hair is gone. Who is this desirable mate again? He crunches his toast wrong and spreads the newspaper across the entire table. She exchanges PMS for menopause while wrinkles rise and body parts fall.

This is when Mrs. Swan takes out her knitting and Mr. Swan needs his arthritis medication. They swim feather to feather into the sunset.

But at the grand old age of 20. Need I say more?

# DyiNg to Laugh

When it comes to dying, there is nothing funny about it. Or like the saying goes, "If it ain't death, I can handle it."

But sometimes you do have to handle it. About death and the stages of dying, I find it inordinately rude behavior of that Death Guy Wearing Black to account for unfinished business, especially to those around the afflicted. They must disrupt their lives, and perhaps finances, to hover around someone whose bio hangs in the balance between decades of life history, and the black wardrobe that follows any day.

But moreover, that Death Guy Wearing Black doesn't understand that most of us don't have time in our busy lives to just up and die. I always said that the Wicked Witches of the Diagnosis People will have to catch up with me for the bad news. Before that, there is simply no time to fool around with such unruly disruptions. I would show my schedule to the Wicked Witches of the Diagnosis People, and say that I have too many goals and accomplishments for such nonsense as minor details like cancer or other deadly interruptions.

My grandmother in her 90's, couldn't stand all the humdrum, "How do you feel?" and with much finality scowled, "scatter" to all around her. I'm thinking, however, that perhaps those glum faces gathering at her bedside might have used a bit of humor, though now that I think of it, those relatives were humorless and more worried about clean houses and folding their hands. Had they known anything about laughter as the best medicine, she might not have banished them from her deathbed. That's the time to use it, after all (along with a few hallucinogenic drugs, of course).

I told that same grandmother while in her 80's when she was having stomach problems that indeed later took her to surgery, "Well grandma, it sounds like you're in labor and about to deliver." For the moment, she scoffed and snapped, "Oh, for mercy sakes!" But for that same moment of comic relief, she felt better, or at least forgot her pain.

And so I approached the bedside of a dying friend the other day. There was nothing funny about the scene where a vivacious, formerly active and healthy person would so swiftly turn into a gray, shapeless puddle sinking into a bed that will soon envelope her last breaths. I was rather startled, in fact, because it was no longer the same friend whose positive and upbeat personality happened to be battling cancer; it was that rude Death Guy Wearing Black standing there and ready to take the wrong young person for no reason at all.

We joked in the beginning when the Wicked Witches of the Diagnosis People first appeared. I told her that it couldn't possibly be so because she was younger, better looking and in better shape than I. I always aspired to be more like her; I would do more exercise, subscribe to health magazines and, well maybe blonde isn't my hair color, but I could still be better about living.

We always assumed that Death Guy Wearing Black would stay away, especially if we just kept laughing. But alas, he was there and when I approached, she managed to barely reach her weak arms upward and say, "hug." (This is where the words before me get a little blurred.) I stroked her hair and her hands telling her about how beautiful she was and how I loved her. She sank back into hazy confusion.

But when I couldn't resist some humor with, "Well, the real problem is that we didn't drink enough wine," she perked right up and laughed. That Death Guy Wearing Black even tittered.

# ACKNOWLEDGEMENTS

I would like to thank Michelle Yeager for a long friendship when I did the yakking and she did the listening. Lifelong friend Cindy Sugerman has provided much fodder for humor as we experienced husbands, divorces, babies and all the laughter necessary to survive such. Ruth Gill and her powerful intellect has provided much material in our friendship that began with ballet class and continues as we watch those same body parts fall.

Thanks to surrounding family, that is the family that still speaks; son Jason who never had a serious thought travel through his mind in his entire life and daughter Piper who diverts all serious thoughts to her husband, Dan. Ex-husband Conrad has always been supportive, though it's complicated. Grandsons Calvin and Connor are too young to know it, but someday they will see themselves in these goofy chapters.

Thank you to Windy City's publishing gals Dawn, Rachel and Lise who have been most patient about my techie failures – not so funny.

Finally, a big thank you to illustrator/designer/artist Krista Wildermuth of New Jersey (krista.wildermuth@gmail.com) for stepping up to a quick deadline because I procrastinate too much. I hope that she continues to make her special talents available in the future if I promise to have a more civilized deadline.

Made in the USA
Charleston, SC
17 October 2011